Leona Storey

SRL Publishing

www.srlpublishing.co.uk

SRL Publishing Ltd
42 Braziers Quay
Bishop's Stortford
Herts, CM23 3YW

First published worldwide by SRL Publishing in 2020

Copyright © Leona Storey 2020

The author reserves the right to be identified as the author of this work

ISBN: 978-1-9163373-1-2

All rights reserved. No part of this publication may be reproduced or transmitted in any form or by any means, electronic, mechanical, photocopying or otherwise, without the prior permission of the publishers.

This book is a work of fiction. Names, characters, places and incidents are either a product of the authors imagination or are used fictitiously. Any resemblance to actual people, living or dead, events or locales, is entirely coincidental.

For anyone who has ever struggled

accepting who they are

Pride

There are a lot of thanks to be given to everyone who read this book in its early stages. Every comment, every question, got it to where it is now, in your hands.

I almost can't believe this has finally happened. It wouldn't be without the support of my partner, Ben, who was there for every single moment of this journey. I will never be able to thank you enough for everything you did throughout the year I wrote this book: the late-night editing, the reassurances, the ability to answer every single one of my insignificant questions… You are a saint, truly, and I love you.

I want to also give thanks to everyone who helped me within my own journey of acceptance. We live in a society surrounded by heterosexuality – we watch it on our TVs, we read it in our books, we hear it in our songs. Learning that you're 'different', that you'll have to 'come out', is terrifying. I particularly want to thank my friend, Anya, for helping me to understand my bisexuality. I also want to thank Eve, who I saw so much of myself within, when she was coming to terms with her sexuality. You are both inspirations to me.

Leona Storey

But, in all, I think my biggest thanks goes to you. By holding this book in your hands, you're helping me achieve the dream I've had since I was a child. I hope that Lucy's story of struggle and acceptance has helped you, whether it be within your own identity or to understand those around you.

Lastly, I urge you to remember – no matter what the homophobes say, or what they do, we will exist. You are never alone in your fight for equality.

1

Rainbow was my favourite colour.

Mum told me that it was cheating to pick rainbow because technically it was seven colours, not one. I didn't care. There was something about those seven colours. The order they were in, the way they blended together. They were something you only ever got to see when the sky poured rain and shine sun at the same time or when the light refracted at a perfect angle. The world had to earn a rainbow.

But Pride was full of them. Rainbows became normal, commonplace, draped across every building and street in Brighton. Flags, streamers and balloons flew through the sky, caught in an end of summer breeze. Some people even wore rainbow clothes, their skin adorned with the paint of bright colours.

Overwhelming was an understatement.

Next to me, her hand clammy as it clung to mine, Brittany's voice was loud in my ear. "Come the fuck on, Lucy! I don't want to miss the main act. There's going to be a Lady Gaga tribute!"

"Since when did you care about that?" I scoffed, letting her pull my arm as we weaved through the crowds. It was nearing the end of August and the thick crowd around us made my skin sticky with sweat.

"Since I overheard someone say that she's going to be wearing a replica of the crazy meat dress!" She explained, pausing to tug up her fishnets. A man bumped into her as she did so. Unaffected, she continued,

"Clearly, it's an unmissable moment in our lives, my dear friend."

"Oh, clearly," I said. "Can't think of why we've never done it before."

"It's a once in a lifetime experience."

We bumped into endless bodies. When we'd gotten off the train that morning, the city had hit me with a sensory overload. The streets were crowded beyond belief, music blasted at the highest volume from every window. Even the rainbows were almost too much.

Standing in my striped shirt and dungarees, plainness oozing, you'd blink and miss me. Everyone seemed to be dripping in extravagance. Beads piled around their necks, party streamers tied into their hair, holographic poufy skirts cinched to their waists.

Pride was full of people who were supposed to be like me. People who had been on the same journey of denial and discovery. People who had spent endless nights awake, trying to work out who they were and accept it. And yet, next to these people, I felt alien. I'd expected to feel a sense of belonging, a community of support, but all I got was a headache.

"Where are we going?" I tried to ask her over the noise.

"Uhh…" Brittany pondered, slowing down to look at the map on her phone. "I've no bloody clue. I think we keep going up this road."

"Oh no. It'll be such a shame if we can't find it…"

She stuck her tongue out at me, her piercing glistened in the early afternoon sun. "Killjoy."

"Come on, Brit. You know I didn't want to go to this thing," I replied.

"Fake Gaga, or Pride?"

I stared at her, hesitant. "Pride."

Sighing, she resumed pulling me down the street. "Can't you let yourself go for once? This is *your* place! *Your* people! *Your* community!"

There was no point arguing against her; she wouldn't understand. She'd slotted in easily with the crowd, her barely-there shorts and glitter covered cheeks making her one of them without actually being one of them. Times like that, I envied of how easily she could let herself go.

I'd pretty much always known that I'm a lesbian but being *out* was still new to me. Endless websites and online forums had shown me the word *'community'* more times than I thought humanly possible but being at Pride made me feel like I was the loser kid at the popular girls' sleepover.

And it wasn't as though I could talk to anyone about it. As much as I loved Brittany, she would never get it. Completely boy-crazy, she was so open about sex that I think even sex itself would like her to keep a few things private.

When I came out, Brittany was ecstatic, breathlessly ranting about the times she'd wanted to point out some supposedly hot girl to me. "But I'd wanted to respect your boundaries, though, you know? I didn't want to pressure you into coming out, but *shit*, Luce! Thank God!" She'd said.

She demanded that we celebrate it by going to Pride in Brighton. Even then, I had no problem showing my reluctance show, but she'd only smiled gleefully me. She always got her way.

Events like Pride were full of drinking and partying and noise. I had more than my fair share of that side of life from Brittany's escapades to know I hated every aspect of it. Still, I'd gone along with it. There was no talking her out of it. In the end, going to Pride was more for her than it was for me.

I'd made myself feel better about the whole thing by telling myself that anything was better than packing up boxes and shifting furniture with my parents all day. I wasn't keen on leaving my childhood home - where I'd taken my first steps and said my first words - but going to Pride was my excuse to forget about all of that for a day.

My parents had been great about my coming out, too. They gave me the spiel that every gay kid wants, telling me that they'd love and accept me no matter who I decided to bring home. It felt fresh out of a *"what do you say to your kid when they come out"* Google search, but I was still appreciative. They still loved me, and I felt lucky for that.

Brittany's uncanny ability to speak louder than a PA system meant that a tonne of kids from school had also already found out. Everyone seemed cool with it. So far, I'd gotten nothing but support. Somewhere deep down, I kind of knew everyone would be fine about it. Everyone that mattered, anyway.

The only thing was that, before I came out, I'd expected it to feel as if a door had opened, one that could lead me to a place where I could just be me. Where I'd feel at home in my skin, not the weird seventeen-year-old lesbian. But for some reason, I still couldn't take a breath without feeling like there was something sticking to my lungs.

"I *think* we're in the right place," she said. She squinted at her phone before shoving it into her pocket and joining a queue of over-excited spectators.

It bustled for a few minutes, people joining behind us, before we all got ushered toward the entrance. When we finally got in, we stood near the back of the hall, facing a stage that was empty apart from gigantic speakers and rainbow flags. Chatter and laughter bounced around the high ceilings, making the place feel desolate, despite the bustling crowd. There were easily a thousand people shoved in this church-like place.

"Are you sure this is the right place?" I asked Brittany. "It doesn't feel very... Gaga-ish."

Brittany shrugged, bracelets on her wrists jangling with her movement. "All we can do is wait, I guess."

Despite the summer air outside, there was a crisp chill inside the hall. Behind us, the entrance door slammed shut. The echo thrusted everyone into momentary silence before they started blabbering once more.

A knot of anxiety took residence in my chest. The atmosphere bubbled with drunken laughter and shouting, but I didn't like it. My skin prickled, hairs standing on end. For a second, I worried about being a dampener to Brittany. I wanted her to have a good time, but me acting like a shaking child couldn't have been any fun.

"Hey, Brit-"

Brittany elbowed my side, interrupting me. "Look, look, look!"

A single multi-coloured strobe spotlight light hit the stage. The black curtains moved slightly, slowly opening as the crowd's chatters turned into celebratory cheers.

I stood on my tip toes, squinting as I attempted to get a glimpse of the tribute act. Beside me, Brittany squealed, her infectious excitement making my knot loosen a little bit. I felt a small smile tug at the ends of my lips. The crowd buzzed, sparking something within me. My body felt the thrum and my voice wanted to cheer along with them all.

In my pocket my phone vibrated, but I ignored it. I was finally starting to have a good time, feeling like I was a part of something, rather than sticking out of it.

We kept waiting, the stage curtains half-open. A minute passed by us, confusion growing the longer we waited. My phone kept on vibrating. It was so insistent it felt like my leg was vibrating with it. I moved to my pocket, giving up my resolve to not look at it when I heard a scream.

It wasn't like the cheers of the crowd, that were getting rowdier with each second they had to wait. It was a little distant, coming from the backstage. I rationalised, passing off the screams someone outside messing about. But then there were more screams, guttural and horrific. The crowd began to quieten, the pumping atmosphere changed.

"W-what was that?" I asked, facing Brittany.

Her sun-kissed face had turned a little paler, her eyes glued to the stage. I wished she would look at me. "I don't know," she said, her voice wobbling like jelly. "Probably just some kids messing about outside."

I nodded, trying to feel convinced.

I dug into my pocket for my phone. I tried to read the texts that were flying onto my screen, but I couldn't lock onto more than a couple of words before being interrupted by phone calls that kept failing after a couple of rings.

Calls and texts and voicemails fought for my attention, but my eyes couldn't focus. I saw my Mum and Dad's contact among the flitting messages. Only a few words stuck out, blaring through foghorns. *Run. Safe. Hide. I love you.*

Unable to tear myself away from the screen, I nudged what I hoped was Brittany's arm. "B-Brit-"

"What, can you see something?"

"No, look-"

Pride

"I can't see anything on the stage!"

"No, look at my pho-"

There was a bang. A noise I'd only ever heard in movies. Then, a man burst through the curtains. The crowd were still cheering, thinking that the concert was starting.

But then we saw his gun. He was so tall, so stocky, but the gun was still the loudest part of him. It was the biggest gun I'd ever seen. The only gun I'd ever seen.

The crowd's cheers contorted into uninhibited screams. Primal, instinctual fear hung in the air.

He fired his first shot, presumably hitting someone at the very front of the crowd. Panic began to ripple at a lightning speed as the sound of the gunfire echoed through the hall. My ears rang, the gunshot louder than I'd ever imagined it being.

Through a bustle of bodies, Brittany's eyes found mine.

Run. Hide. The words echoed through my brain like fireflies.

I pushed through people, grabbed her hand and turned to the entrance door behind us, but everyone else had the same idea. I watched as people pulled on the handles, in pain as they pushed their muscles, but it wouldn't budge.

The gunman kept shooting at the front of the crowd. Wails filled the hall. Eyes helplessly stared, frozen in shock. A small group were spurred by the ricocheting sounds, pushing to open the doors, banging and screaming for help. He shouted back at us, but his words drowned in the noise. I only heard one thing he said: *faggot scum*.

Barely able to breathe against the force of the bodies around me, my muscles trembled, adrenaline filling my blood. My instincts told me to move, but there was nowhere to go.

More shots. More screams. I clutched Brittany tighter, my knuckles whitening.

The gunman shouted. I couldn't hear him, but the tone of his voice felt so clearly laced with hatred. Anything he said was drowned out by the terrified begging and pleading of the lives below him and the pounding of the gunfire.

He jumped down from the stage and walked over the dead and dying bodies as if they were nothing more than dirt on his shoes. An inconvenience.

Desperation tugged at every instinct I had as he got closer and closer to joining us. At his emergence in the crowd, everyone pushed harder at the doors. People were forced together, crushed into spaces that weren't there. I struggled against the tide of bodies as Brittany's hand slipped out of mine.

"No!" I screamed.

"Lucy! Lucy!"

I felt her fingers scratch at my arms, sharp fake nails clutching my arm. I couldn't feel the pain as they dug crescents into my skin, drawing blood to the surface, desperate not to let go of me.

The gunman kept firing. People kept screaming. Brittany kept digging.

Warm, fresh blood dripped down my arm. My ears rang, reeling from the sheer volume of the gunfire at such a close range. The pressure of the crowd kept pushing against me.

Beside me, a woman jolted, hit by a bullet. A splatter of her blood hit me and mixed with my own.

The constriction of the crowd stopped her falling. She was limp, held up by the wall of people. Her bright ginger hair jiggling. Dead, but still standing.

I knew I was screaming but I couldn't hear it. My lungs had become black holes. My eyes were transfixed on the stream of dark blood that left the ginger woman's chest. It was such a small hole, a gunshot wound, but all I could imagine was metal ripping through skin, twisting through her heart.

That woman could have been me. It could have been Brittany. There was no difference between us except from where we stood.

A blinding light hit my face. It took me a second to realise it was daylight. The doors had opened.

The doors had opened!

Pressure lifted off my crushed body as people flooded through them. My brain started to clear. We might survive this, all we had to do was get out of those doors.

I reached out for Brittany, but she wasn't clinging on my arm anymore. I hadn't even noticed, but only the crescent shaped gouges from her fingernails were left.

"Brittany! Brittany!" I cried out, my frantic eyes scanning over faces that all looked blurred in my panic.

The gunman began to shoot with abandon, realising he was about to lose control of us. People piled out of the doors, pushing me as they did so. The animal part of me, the one controlling the instinct and adrenaline, screamed at me to leave. Run out of the doors with the rest of the crowd. But I couldn't, not until I'd found Brittany.

Sirens outside started to blare. Between each wail, the gunman released a bullet.

I pushed against the crowd, trying to weave in and out of the people. The effort of it was exhausting. Some of the dead bodies that had been amongst us fell to the ground as others ran.

Another person fell, hit by a bullet in the shoulder. I tried to look for Brittany's pink hair, normally the first thing you'd see in any crowd. But not at Pride. Here, she just sunk into the sea of people.

My foot caught on something and I fell to my knees. The force of the escaping crowd pushed me until I hit the floor, my head striking the tiled floor. Blaring white hit the corners of my vision.

I tried to haul myself up, but the crowd wouldn't relent. My body was flat against the floor. The people didn't care. Didn't even notice. I was another unfeeling dead body.

My ears were still ringing, the sound around me muffled, but the sirens were getting louder, closer. I wanted to scream for help, but stars, buoyant, swimming across my eyes, kept coming back as feet knocked into my skull.

I tried to look at the shoes passing by me, over me. I couldn't see Brittany's trademark Doc Martens. Even if I did, there was nothing to say they would be hers.

All I could see were blurred movements. A foot stood on my arm, the full weight of the body it belonged to crushing my bones. I wasn't sure I could even feel the pain.

Then I noticed her. Lying. The woman who died next to me. Some of her ginger hair had been ripped out by the force of the stampede. Her eyes stuck out to me. A beautiful, fresh green. Summer grass green.

I thought about how someone somewhere, was in love with those eyes. Then the stars took over.

2

I've never liked that smell.

It invades your nose, burning off the little hairs inside it. It's in every doctor's office, so I eat an apple a day. It's in every dentists, so I floss extra hard.

And, it's in every hospital.

And, that's why I never should have gone to Pride.

I had three days in a hospital bed to come to the conclusion that this could've been much worse.

Seventeen dead and even more injured. Everyone seemed keen to tell me that I was lucky. I could've been dead. There's nothing worse than being dead, I could hear them think.

I couldn't help but scoff. This wasn't *luck*.

Taking up space, I let the sympathy wash over me. They were right; I was still here. Alive. No gunshot wounds, but a broken arm and a mild concussion.

To them, I was poor victim. It broke their hearts. But to me, the only thing I was a victim of was bad balance.

Every night since I'd been admitted, my parents slept by my hospital bed, crumpled up in uncomfortable chairs. They would wake up, complaining of cricked necks and achy backs.

I wanted to tell them to go home. Unfiltered amounts of time with my parents stuck in the children's ward of a hospital was a recipe for even more murders, I felt.

If I were only a couple months older, I'd be eighteen and in the adults ward. I wouldn't be surrounded by children crying for their parents, bored and complaining about the crappy kids shows on TV.

I was glad that Brittany wasn't here with me. She'd been pushed out the back doors with the crowd, getting a few bruises and scratches along the way. Some paramedic had taken her to an ambulance, sitting with her while she waited for her parents to pick her up. She'd texted, joking that he totally was eyeing her up.

She was only trying to make me smile, but I couldn't find it within me to text back. I imagined her with yellow and purple bruises flowering her pale skin. A middle-aged guy wrapping a shock blanket over her shoulders, helpless.

I promised myself that I'd text her when I got back home. She wasn't allowed to come down to the hospital to visit me. Her parents worried it would be too much to handle. Seeing Brighton and the busy hospital wards full of people who could've easily been her.

My dad was sitting in one of the two chairs next to the bed, flicking through a newspaper. "Says here that the guys mother always knew that he disagreed with the gay lifestyle."

My mum tutted. I rolled over to face the curtain.

I tried to close my eyes. To block the swirls and bright colours that plastered the children's ward. As if all these colours could help anyone forget where they were and why they were here.

It was a sinfully boring place. Despite only being weeks away from legally classifying as an adult, I wasn't allowed to go wandering to the adult ward to see what they had. The only entertainment was a TV was in the common room. Even that got locked in a little cage so you couldn't flick the channels. The common room was also full of books and magazines and varying toys, but it was all for kids. I wasn't a kid.

I wish I was a kid.

"There's an interview with her, too. An exclusive one." Dad continued.

"Really? Pass it over, I'll have a read," Mum said.

"Can't believe she agreed to it."

"Well, why wouldn't she? She probably wanted to distance herself from what her son did. As much as she can, anyway."

"Yes. Gives her a chance to tell her story."

"Mmm, true. Very true."

"Well, even with this interview, she's still going to be seen as-"

I bolt upright, tired of their scripted chit-chat. I'd heard endless variations of the same conversation played for the last three days. "Will you shut up about the guys stupid mother already?"

They try to hide that I've hurt them, but it's written so plainly across their faces. It may as well be dancing across the room, shimming maracas and singing Les Mis. They nod like compliant little puppies, sitting on the very edges of their seats. Every movement ignites more irritation.

Throwing the scratchy thin blankets over me as I lie down, I roll back to face the curtain. I try to ignore the pain that etches up my broken arm, but I can't stop grimacing. I'm glad that they can't see me. They'd want to comfort me, hug me, hold me. Stifle me.

I know I shouldn't be so snappy with them. I loved my parents. They loved me. They have always been so supportive of me. When I was eight and wanted to be a baker, they found an Easy Bake oven, getting it shipped all the way from the US to here. When I was thirteen and I became obsessed with *The Hunger Games*, they bought me my own little bow and arrow set. When I came out, they hugged me and assured me that they were so happy I was able to be myself with them.

They weren't doing anything wrong, and they didn't deserve me being a brat to them. It was just me. New Lucy. A Lucy that snaps. A Lucy that's cranky. A Lucy that's irritable and unfiltered and tired and hates everyone around her for breathing.

That's the Lucy who's been here since the shooting. Infiltrating my body.

I was a little scared she's always been here. This version of me. Lying under the surface, watching, waiting. A backbone waiting to grow.

I was a little scared that I liked her.

My parents have never needed to discipline me. And because I'm their only child, I guess they've forgotten how the whole discipline thing works.

I've always been Miss. Good, Miss. Average, if I'm being honest. Consistent B grades. Even A's sometimes, if I pushed myself a little harder. Not much of a drinker or a party animal. Never really tried to commit to a sport or an instrument. Befriending Brittany was probably the most rebellious and out of the ordinary thing I've ever done... She got a nose ring at age thirteen and hasn't stopped poking holes in her body ever since. She's been the only variable in my otherwise starting-scene-of-a-movie life.

A sigh went through me. Travelling from my lungs and spreading outwards and filling me with stifled energy. "I'm going for a walk," I told them both. It wasn't like me to make such sweeping declarations. I've always been the type to get permission. To tell my parents every detail of where I was going, who I was going with, what I'd be doing.

"I... Will you be okay?" My mum asked.

Pride

"Well, let's see... I broke my arm, not my legs. I'm pretty sure the doctors would know if I had concussion by now. Oh, and I didn't get shot and die like a bunch of other people," I said. "So yeah, I think I'll be fine walking down the hall for two minutes."

I swung my legs off the bed, cradling my arm as I walked off. My parents didn't follow. It wasn't surprising. I'd become Medusa, and if they talked to me for long enough, they'd probably become stone.

Everywhere was buzzing. Too alive. Too loud. There was something bubbling and fizzing under my skin and around my extremities. Without thinking, I let my fingers drift to the crescent-shaped scabs on my arms. Brittany had first caused them after clinging onto me in the arena hall, but they were now changing. Forming to my fingernail shape. Every time I felt this perpetual knot of on-edginess, I let my fingers dig into the shapes. For some reason, the pain stopped the fizzing. It brought me back a tiny bit. For a moment, the only thing I could feel was the pain that I was causing.

I dawdled made my way to the common room. I didn't need to look at the signs anymore. After being sentenced to spend at least a week in the hospital, I had been building a little map of this place in my head.

The common room wasn't far. Two rights, a left, through the pair of glass doors, a cursory walk past the nurses station and you were there. It was for children's ward patients only, but most of them never bothered going in. They were either too sick or their parents were bringing in other fun stuff to waste their time away with.

Today, there were three other people in there. One was a young girl, no older than 10, with a bandanna half-tied round her bald head, reading a copy of Matilda. Another was a very young girl, playing with a falling-apart train track set. It seemed to be that she pretending that the trains were fairies instead of vehicles. Her mother was watching her, drinking in the pure imagination dripping off the girl. Savouring it. A ball of ice formed in my throat.

The other person was a boy. He seemed to be around my age, maybe a little younger. It was hard to tell. What I could tell, however, is that he wouldn't stop smiling at me. The *Horrible Histories* book he was flicking through when I'd walked in was now on his lap with a finger tucked between the pages to keep his place. He noticed my stare and stumbled to find his page again, a slight pink tinge visible against his pale skin.

I broke my gaze and walked past him, going straight to the TV area full of bean bags and cushioned chairs. They were miles comfier than the slab of wood they called a bed back in my hospital room. Easing myself down, being careful not to knock my casted arm, I slipped into a bright yellow bean bag. It was obnoxious and bright, but it was one of the few that hadn't got vomit or blood stains on it. I wondered how often they replaced these things. If they even could with the shitty amounts of money that hospitals get.

With my good arm, I started to flip through the assortment of kids magazines in the rack next to me. They were all plastered with bright-smiling tweens and stock images of internet personalities. I settled on the one that tells me it will be able to predict what my future husband will be like. Fat chance.

I tried to engross myself with the question of whether I agreed that '*redhead Prince Harry is a total BABE!*', but I was too aware of the boy. Out of my peripheral vision, I could see him trying to inconspicuously get a glance of me. It took a couple of feigned interest page turns for the boy to brave the questionably stained bean bag next to me.

After what felt like a forever of awkward silence, twisting his fingers, he finally introduced himself. "I'm Nathan." He said, closing the book on his lap.

Despite his obvious nerves, his voice was all chipper. Bright. It made my head hurt. I turned another page, ignoring him. This time, it was first date fashion advice from a blonde B-Lister who likely had no affiliation with the magazine whatsoever.

"Looks pretty interesting. Can I have a look?"

He leaned over my shoulder, his arm touching my own. On instinct, I jerked backwards. Some beanbag fluff puffed out, unprepared for my sudden movements. Nathan raised his eyebrows at me.

"I get it," he said, holding his hands up. "I'm pretty protective over my copies of… *'Go Girlz!'* too."

A breath of laughter escaped me. For a second, it felt as though the new cold and cynical exterior I'd been building since what happened at Pride had broken down by some sort of sunshine.

"Quick, someone call a nurse, I think your ice queen exterior is melting!" Nathan noticed.

With some effort, I painted my face plain once more. "Hilarious."

"She speaks!"

"She won't if you keep acting like an asshole." I retorted, finally breaking my gaze away from the magazine. His eyes were a deep brown-black. They steeply contrasted from the sandy-lightness that was his hair. I could tell from the lines creasing around his mouth that he wore this grin a lot. Even old Lucy, pre-being-shot-at Lucy, wouldn't have been able to imagine being so happy in life.

Nathan shrugged. "My apologies," he said, not looking the least bit sorry at all. "What's your name?"

"You know, it's funny - I actually came in here for a bit of peace and quiet. Would you believe it?" I asked.

"Really? Peace and quiet? In here?" He scoffed. The TV blaring out an old episode of *Tracy Beaker*. There was a kid crying after having broken some of the train tracks she was playing with. Faintly, an endless beeping of machines and phone trilling's from the corridor.

I relented. "I'm Lucy."

"And why are you in the hospital, Lucy?"

I sucked in some air as an image struck me, cold and from nowhere. It was dark, crowded, dusty and overbearing. My lungs began to falter. Somewhere behind me, a screaming so loud it broke through my vision.

Nathan was staring at me, a quizzical eyebrow raised. Or maybe it was concern. I didn't know. I didn't know what had happened. Where I'd gone. I looked behind me, searching for the source of the screaming, but nothing had changed around me.

I thought I heard Nathan speak, but his voice sounded muffled and foggy. It was only when he tried to touch my arm that I seemed to break out of my own cloud. I lurched away from his touch once more. The simplicity of his palm, rough and encompassing, was suffocating.

"Jesus, what's it to you? Who are you? Why are you even talking to me?" I snapped.

"I-I'm sorry," Nathan stumbled. For the first time since meeting him, his smile broke. Somewhere inside me, it made the anger bubble burst, frightened at the hurt I'd caused. The power that I'd had, and how I'd used it.

"No, God, no, I'm sorry, I…" I stammered, tripping over my own words. I'd hurt my parents, and now I'd hurt this boy. I felt like a sharp spiked stick, prodding and splintering at anyone who tried to get close.

Pride

"No, it's fine. I'm sorry I disturbed you. I should've known hospitals weren't a good place to talk to a cute girl." He said with the same jokiness sneaking its way back into his voice.

I forced a smile. I imagined a hand reaching down inside me, trying to find a scrap of the old Lucy still lingering somewhere. I didn't know how convincing my smile was, but it must've been enough for Nathan, who smiled back without hesitation. "I don't mean to be so cranky. It's been a tough few days." I explained.

"I get that. Hospitals suck."

"To say the least."

A silence passed by us, quiet and still, feeling larger than it was. His words beat their way around my skull: *cute girl, cute, girl, a girl who's cute, girl, cute girl...*

It was stupid. I'm gay. There was no point of him hitting on me. I'm a lesbian. I'm so lesbian that I went to Pride. I was almost a dead lesbian at Pride. I wished I'd never gone to Pride. I wished I didn't come out. I wished that none of this was even happening.

"I should be getting back. My brothers coming in the next lot of visiting hours and I want to get a real good nap in before that," Nathan said.

I looked up at him. Picture perfect. A million girls would dream of this moment. A funny boy. A kind boy. One with wavy California dream hair and eyes felt like taking a long walk in a dark, enchanted woods. What would it be like, I wondered, to be one of those girls? Butterflies swarming in my stomach, lips withering to be kissed? What would it to be like to want those things from a boy, and not a girl? To not have that make you stand out so much?

"Sure," I said. "I'll see you around."

"Actually you won't. I'm getting discharged tomorrow," he said. "Turns out you don't need a bed for a long time after saying goodbye to your appendix."

I gave a small snicker. "Well, good luck. And I'm sorry. Still."

"Don't be," he said effortlessly, as if it was that easy to not feel something. "And look - if you're still feeling that bad, you could make it up to me with one simple thing."

I looked bemused. "That sounds creepy. How old are you again? Is this the sort of weird behaviour what my parents warned me about from men?"

Nathan relaxed, the banter easing the memory of my anger. "All I'm asking is, if you might ever want to chat to me again, is that you add me on Facebook or something."

"Seriously? Facebook?"

"Well, I can't remember my phone number off by heart unlike I can my own name." he explained with a faux defensiveness.

"Impressive," I said. "Fine. I'll add you on Facebook, grandpa."

His smile reached almost dangerous levels of teeth-showing. I'd need to whack out a pair of sunglasses around this guy every time I said something even kind of nice.

"Look up Nathan Huxley. I'm the one that goes to Hove Boys Grammar School," he said. "My profile picture is me holding a big fish. That should help you find the right one."

"A big fish?" I asked.

"I like fishing."

"No shit."

"I hope to talk to you soon, Lucy. See you."

"Bye, fish boy." I said, giving him a wave as he turned to go. He returned my goodbye with a signature smile, leaving the room 750 watts brighter than it was before.

# 3

After a year-long week, I was discharged from the hospital under strict instructions not to drink, take recreational drugs or do any sort of strenuous exercise. I'd struggled not to laugh in the doctors faces, imaging a Brittany-ised version of myself, platform shoes dangling from one hand and a stubby cigarette in the other.

I'd never minded our differences too much, not understanding the appeal of Brittany's lifestyle. I watched, over the years of our friendship, as she changed; taking up wild drinking on Saturday nights instead of watching *The X Factor*.

She never pressured me, either. She'd offer, I'd say no, and she'd look at me like she couldn't understand me either. But that was always it.

"Why do you like the whole… you know, party and clubs stuff?" I'd asked her one particularly hungover morning after she'd stumbled into my house at dawn and fallen asleep in my bed. I'd poked her awake at ten, wafting my signature for-Brittany-only Hugs'n'Hangovers sandwich in front of her nose. Not only did it get served with a hug, but the bacon hugged the sausages too.

Tentative and riding a wave of alcohol-induced nausea, Brit took a bite. "It just relaxes me, I guess," she mumbled, half-way through chewing, bits of bacon fat getting stuck on the ball of her tongue piercing. I grimaced.

"But *how*? Being in those places just makes me more anxious."

"That's 'cus you're not drinking."

I rolled my eyes. "You know I don't want to."

"Well, Luce, that's the secret to enjoying these parties," she said as she took a bigger, braver bite of my sandwich. "Getting drunk! I like getting drunk, so I like the parties. I like the clubs."

A beat passed between us as I tossed this over in my mind. Alcohol always tasted like shit to me.

Brittany turned closer to me, closing the gap between us. "You know you don't have to ever come to these things," she reassured me. "I'd never be mad or anything."

"I know. I just wish I knew what I was missing out on."

"Honestly, it's nothing special. It always smells like sweat," she said. "Besides, the truth is, I only ever get drunk so I can have your *wonderful* breakfasts in the morning."

I smiled and let her pull me in for a hug, kissing the top of my head, but the words didn't comfort me. I was always being told that nothing was ever *anything special*. That I wasn't missing out on anything at all. When I was younger, it was school proms that I'd be too afraid to go to without a date, and I sure as hell didn't want to bring a boy. Now I was getting older, it was house parties that were full of horny teenagers and getting drunk in parks on a Tuesday.

Since then, I started to go to fewer and fewer parties with Brittany. I didn't feel as guilty anymore, even if I still felt like I was missing some essential part of growing-up. Instead, I stayed at home, in the comfort and familiarity of the room I'd lived for longer than I could remember.

Knowing I'd get to go back home was the only thing that kept me going through my stay at the hospital.

Everything about my home comforted me. Stepping through the front door after that week felt like slipping into an old pair of pyjamas, worn but warm. For a moment, being in my home, it felt as though a part of myself had come back. A part of myself that I hadn't felt since Pride.

Mum closed the front door behind us, and I walked through the old hallway. It was thin and somewhat rickety from the years of plastering over cracks and holes. Endless photos of family members, from my Great Aunt Bethany to my Australian cousins, lined the faded orange painted walls. At the end of the hall sat an overly large, open-roofed tank housing one little goldfish.

"Hello again, Brucie." I tapped the top of his water, causing the water to ripple. He swam up to meet me, his little mouth kissing my fingertip, the white tips of his fins sparkling under the fluorescent light. I sprinkled an extra heaping of his flakes as an apology for being gone so long. I was sure my parents would've fed him, but I didn't want him to forget that he loved me the most. People who say fish can't love clearly never met Brucie.

Mum and Dad squeezed themselves by me, getting into the kitchen. I shifted my backpack, giving them room, before following them in.

One thing I loved about the house was how bright it was. Every room seemed to have a colour. The kitchen was a lemony yellow. The cupboards and trimmings were all white, but everything from the tiles to the fake-marble counters shouted sunshine. The floor was made of smooth tiles. Often, in the summers, I'd lay half-naked on the kitchen floor; it was the only part of the house that stayed cool. It sucked in the winter, though, when even the fluffiest of my bed socks couldn't keep out the freezing cold touch.

"Got enough teacups there to make us all a cuppa?" Dad asked.

My Mum opened the cupboard above the kettle. Normally, you'd find an endless mis-matched Jenga pile of mugs in there, collected over years of gone-by Christmases and birthdays.

But now, there were only two mugs. On the dark and dusty shelf, they looked a little lonely. Everything else packed in some box somewhere. Or worse, thrown into a skip.

"Only two, I'm afraid," Mum replied, hooking the handles of both with her index fingers, swaying them gently. "Went a bit mad and had a cull of all the crockery right before…"

They both turned to look at me. Her words bounced off the walls, ricocheting into the ones that didn't know how to be said. It wasn't enough that my life seemed to have split into a *before* and *after* of the shooting, but now my parents' lives were too.

"It's fine. I don't want a tea, anyway." I said, my eyes finding the floor. I pulled off my trainers, one foot after another, not bothering to undo the laces like I usually would.

A quiet settled over the kitchen. I still felt the words everywhere. On instinct, I reached to the fingernail grooves in my arm. Hardly aware I was even doing it, I was shocked at how I'd managed to form this habit so easily. An uneasiness spread across me as I dug into the scabbed skin right in front of my parents. The scabs came away easily, barely healed from the last time I did this, and the warmth of the first few drops of blood spread underneath my own fingernails. I knew I couldn't keep doing this. At least not in such a visible, open place. They knew that Brittany had caused the first indentations, but they would worry if it wasn't healing.

You'll just have to start doing it somewhere they can't see.

I couldn't shake the thought. After it had intruded, it seemed to be all that I could think. I didn't know where it had come from, or why, but it scared me. I didn't understand how I could have such a harmful thought about my own self. My own skin.

I didn't want to linger on it, to let it take over. I stopped digging and placed my palm over the grooves. Sure, it wasn't exactly the most sanitary thing to do, but I had to quell the bleeding somehow. I could clean them later, or just let the cuts heal on their own. I didn't have to do this.

But you do deserve them, after all.
STOP!

With my good arm, I slammed the palm of my fist on the kitchen counter. My own words reverberated inside my head.

My parents stared at me inexplicably. Their faces contorted into concern and something else that I could only register as fear. They both came toward me, arms outreached, hands open, but I stepped back, flinching. It was as if I was in a car, dangling off a cliff. They were trying to reach for the old Lucy who was stuck inside, but every movement made the car shake and shudder, cracks appearing beneath their feet.

"Sorry," I mumbled. A moment passed, no one quite sure how to react to me.

"You might not want the tea, but you sure do *need* it!" my Dad said, unable to keep the pitch change in his voice hidden.

"Yes, tea fixes all woes!"

"Yeah," I snorted. "I bet those nineteen people who got shot would've been all fine and dandy if only they'd had a cuppa."

I left the kitchen. I didn't want to see their faces. Talking back was not Lucy-style. I was the good girl: the one who helped with grocery shopping and always visited grandma and did her homework. Not the one who made snarky comments to undeserving parents.

I stood by the staircase, clinging onto the old wooden frame. It wobbled in my hand slightly, not able to bare my full weight anymore. Eventually, the silence that I'd left behind me dissipated. My parents switched on the kettle, letting it rumble into to life. They didn't talk about me.

Skipping the third step that always made a loud creak, I walked up the stairs. The upstairs hallway was narrow and long, just like the downstairs. The only difference was that this one was lined with a plaster railing that Mum had always hated it. "Dusty and ugly and damn near impossible to paint over," she'd always say.

As a kid, though, I'd loved it. Slick and agile, I'd hook the tips of my fingers on the edge and swing across the landing. Afternoons after school spent with Brittany, seeing who could think of the best way to get across without letting your feet touch the ground. We even kept it up as we got older, our growing arms and legs providing new challenges to the game.

I thought about how I would never get to play that game again. By the time my broken arm had healed, we'd have moved to a new house. We were moving only five streets away, but it wasn't like I'd ever be able to come back to this place to swing on the banisters again.

At the end of the hall was my room. The door had a jagged square hole near bottom that you could see through, courtesy of Brittany and her bad cutting skills. When I was thirteen, I was desperate a cat for Christmas despite my Dad's allergy. Brittany had taken this to mean "please make a cat flap in my door to convince my Dad he won't die if we get a cat". My parents had been pissed off, but they were too polite to tell her off. When we'd gotten a bit older, it became a too fond of a memory for my parents to even want to change the door.

Besides, what was the point of buying a new bedroom door when we were going to move to a new house one day?

It sucked. My heart felt heavy. There was no way to savour my last few weeks here when I knew I was leaving. It was my home. Every inch of wall, ceiling and floor was familiar to me in a way I didn't even know how to appreciate.

I didn't even understand *why* we had to move. Mum and Dad loved the area we were in. It was outside of London enough for it to be quiet and peaceful, but easy to get into the city for Dad's work. A nice, friendly area with those village-like qualities: local shopkeepers who knew your name and what paper you bought on a Sunday, nice schools with pleasant teachers and Friday night karaoke in the locals-only pub.

That's why they wanted to stay in the same place, even if I didn't understand the point of moving five minutes down the road. It all felt like such a waste of time.

"This house is old and falling apart, Lucy," Mum had said to me one evening over dinner, sometime in the past fortnight. "The new house is one of those new-builds. High speed Wi-Fi and a shower that won't go hot and cold every thirty seconds. It will be nice. Better than this old janky place."

I stroked the wall beside my door, a peeling piece of paint coming off in my hand as I remembered her words, *old janky place*. "Don't worry," I whispered to the wall. "I think you're beautiful."

My door opened, groaning as usual. The air was thick and dusty. I was a perpetual window closer, afraid of bugs and hating the cold. Still, I opened it, letting the ending of August warm air filter through hoping it would sweep out the somewhat damp smell that had flourished in my absence. The breeze, for once, felt nice. Freeing.

Collapsing onto the bed, I threw my backpack down behind me, letting it fall onto the floor. With only two bedrooms in the house, this one had always been mine. Painted and re-painted, wallpapered and de-wallpapered, a thousand times over. For the last four years, it had been a light shade of green with one wall papered with white polka dots. It wasn't my *favourite* makeover of all the years, but it felt so beautifully familiar. A mark of my teen years.

I lay myself into the queen-sized bed, the springs groaning with age while I groaned with relaxation, adoring the luxury of my well-loved duvet and mattress, the pillows that had shaped to my head. My Mum had bought all-new bedding to go with us to the new house. I resented them already, even though the feathers in my own pillows fell out every time I tried to change the cover.

I rolled over onto my good arm, leaving the one in the cast weighing heavily on my side. Closing my eyes against the golden afternoon light, I listened to the sound of the outside. Birds still enjoying the summer warmth chirped. I wondered how they ever managed to leave their homes every year, fleeing south for the winter. Did they care? Did their babies even remember?

Cars drove by and light breezes bustled my curtains. Children played outside, laughing. One of them let out a bloodcurdling scream. *I don't know why they do that*, I thought to myself, *it's not like any of them will ever get murdered.*

Unless they're gay, of course, my own voice muttered back, harsh and ugly. Bitter.

I grimaced. Not even in my room could I find sanctuary.

A second of silence passed, blissful, only to be interrupted by a knocking at the front door. No, a pounding. It could only be Brittany.

I heard the muffled voice of my Dad saying hello, how are you, yes, she's upstairs... before she bounded up the stairs, not bothering to miss out the third step. The creak made me wince, like nails on a chalkboard.

My door swung open. "Hello!" she said, her voice loud, filling the room, the house, the entire street.

I opened one of my eyes. "Hi."

"Oh come on. Get up. You're back! Yay!"

"Hmm, yeah. I'm back after I could've died. Yay."

Brittany sighed and grabbed my good arm, pulling me upright. "Well, firstly, it was *we* could've died, not *I*. But I'll let it slip for I am the bestest of best friends," she said.

I grumbled, a tinge of guilt running through me. I hadn't even bothered to ask how she was, let alone to text her to tell her I was back. My Mum must've. I was selfish. I was disgusting. I wouldn't be winning the *bestest of best friends* title anytime soon.

"And secondly," Brittany continued, "Is that I have brought things to celebrate the wonderful return of my best friend. You have been AWOL for too long. I've missed you."

After a moment of vulnerability, her eyes boring into mine, she pulled away to open her bag. She revealed what would be a doctor's nightmare. It wasn't the drugs or the alcohol that my actual doctors had warned me to stay away from for a while, but it was likely a close second. Jumbo sized bags of Wotsits, Dairy-Milk bars, full-fat Coke and extra-salted popcorn.

"I've got my pyjamas ready in my bag *and* that new Jennifer Lawrence movie because she is so very hot," Brittany said, wiggling her eyebrows up at me. "Truly, I've gone all out for you."

"Yeah, you have," I said.

My voice was small against hers. My whole body felt small. How could she be so… *fine*? In her texts – of which there were many – she had put on a front. I'd thought to myself that when I saw her, she'd likely be real with me. As different as we were, we'd known each other since we were just toddlers in nursery school. If there was anyone she could let her guard down with, it was me.

Maybe she just wanted normalcy, but I didn't know how to do that. The food seemed like mush. Before everything, a night like this with Brittany was all I ever wanted. I loved sharing my space with her. I loved how, as eccentric and as extroverted as she was, she never tired me out. We would watch movies, play board games with all the rules gone wrong, eat the crappiest of crap food. Most of all, we would laugh and laugh and laugh and laugh until Mum told us to please keep the noise down.

I didn't know where to find the part of me again. Looking across from Brittany now, all I saw was a girl trying to reach out to someone who wasn't there. A girl desperate for just one normal night. But her hair, now a dazzling shade of berry red, was too loud. The platform boots on my bed were too big. Her piercings too shiny.

My chest felt full of water. If she didn't go, if she didn't leave right now, I was going to throw up.

"I'm sorry, Brit," I started. "I… I'm just not really in

the mood, I guess."

She softened. "I know. It's hard. But this might make you feel a little normal?"

Normal. I scoffed at the idea of it. What did that word even mean? Normal people didn't go around worrying about random bangs outside actually being gunshots.

I tried to keep the bile from rising to my throat. "I don't think so."

Brittany's face contorted, sad, as she reached over to sling an arm over my shoulder. Just like with Nathan, my body jerked slightly, not wanting to be touched. Her hand lay on me for a second and my muscles tensed so tightly in response. Her face broke, a split second of real hurt manifesting through a frown.

"OK," she said, a breath shakily leaving her core as she took her hand off me. "I guess I'll head off then." She shuffled across the bed, my sheets rustling with the movement, until there was at least half of a metres gap between us. To others, it would've been nothing, but to us, it felt like the Pacific.

"I... I'm really sorry, I just-"

Brittany nodded. "I don't like leaving you when you're not OK."

A beat passed between us before I spoke again. "I am OK."

It was the first lie, the first of so many I'd go on to tell. It wasn't believed by either of us, but I'd soon get better at it. Practise makes perfect.

Brittany took in my face, which I'd made every effort to keep stoic. "I get it," she said. "You need some time or whatever. Being in the hospital for that long can't have helped."

"Mmm."

"Just, text me if you need me OK? I'm still your best friend," she stood up, picking some of the spilt-out sweets and crisps back into the plastic carrier bag. "And… and I need you, too, y'know."

Guilt prickled inside me, dripping down like icy water. I nodded.

"See you soon."

Clamouring, I forced myself up off my bed to open my door for her. Everything felt so off, like a jumper that had been put on backwards, or shoes on the wrong feet.

Just as Brit was about to leave, she reached into the carrier bag and threw the jumbo-bag of Wotsits at me. I caught them, but barely, the foil packaging slipping on the sweaty palm of my good arm.

"Good catch," she said, a ghost of a smile haunting the corners of her lips.

I tried to smile back, but the joke fell flat as the door clicked shut. My broken arm was just another reminder. I listened, her footsteps less full as they bounded down the old stairs. Throwing the Wotsits over to the short distance of my bed, I put my ear against the door, hearing the latch of the front door close behind her.

And just like that, the space between us became real and physical. I didn't know how to close it; I didn't know how to give Brittany what she needed. I was becoming selfish, and I wanted to stop, but it felt like selfish was the only thing I knew how to be. Self-preservation.

My bed pulled me in again, warmth and comfort spilt on the covers. Leaning over, I stuck my phone charger in the only good socket I had left in the room. The rest had all broken somehow or been defiled by some sort of electrical experiments Brittany and I played as kids. It was a wonder neither of us had been killed.

Yeah, you can say that again.
Shut up.

I was thankful for the interruption as my phone

buzzed back into life. I stooped into the sheets, sinking beneath the duvet, the largeness enveloping me. There was something about sticking your head underneath blankets that was immediately calming. Everything went dark as I pulled them over me until I pushed a button on my phone, the blue light lighting my face.

The first thing I did was open Brittany's messages. The last few texts she'd sent me to blurred on the screen, grey bubbles filling the screen. I blinked hard, making them come back into focus. The last text was her telling me she was on her way over. I started to tap out a message, an apology, but my fingers hovered over the keyboard, not knowing which letters to press.

Annoyance crept inside me, it sat in my chest. I wanted to throw the phone away, in disbelief that I had no idea how to talk to my best friend anymore. Instead, I deleted the words. I imagined her for a second, watching our screen, the typing dots disappearing, not knowing if or when they'd reappear.

I closed her messages, exiting the app. I couldn't face her. I couldn't face anything real. So instead, I went to something completely not real. Something so removed from the reality of *before*, that they barely knew who I was, let alone anything about Pride or Brittany or our house move.

I opened the Facebook app and typed in his name: *Nathan Huxley*.

At the top of the page, there he was. That blonde hair and that big fish. Before I lost the nerve, I hit *'message'*.

Hi. It's Lucy from the hospital. Just saying hi.

It sounded as awkward as I felt. But after it sent, all I could think was that he was right about one thing: it *was* a really big fish.

*

It starts not with a bang, but with a gunshot.

I see her there. I don't know where we are, but my hands weave through her hair, my lips on hers. I've never kissed anyone with ginger hair. I've never actually kissed anyone.

But here I am, in this unknown place, kissing this girl who, somehow, I know. Her hair is soft. Impossibly soft. I imagine it being ripped out and used to make a fur coat. No one would know the difference.

She pulls back from the kiss, and I find myself careening toward her. She smirks at me, beckoning, her eyes glinting with fire and fun. My body is lighting up, a catacomb of energy inside that wants her. Needs her.

I move to kiss her neck, the glow of her summer grass green eyes passing by me. Her skin is even softer than her hair. If it got trampled on, it could be ground to dust. It's so supple, bending to my will. Goosebumps follow the trail of my kisses, low moans escaping her lips.

This girl is taking the title of my first kiss. I don't know her name, but I'm not going to stop. I'm aching for her. Magnetised. Pulling apart is unthinkable, so I keep kissing her skin. There is no other choice. It feels too good.

Her moans grow louder, longer. I bathe in them. The more there are, the more pleasure I take and the faster my kisses become. I become confident, venturing south and beyond. I feel so powerful, so in control.

The air around us gets hotter. Her skin gets hotter. I get hotter. I am sure that we are going to set alight. Each kiss becomes an explosion. She moans louder, louder, louder until she is screaming.

For a second, it's okay. I keep my trail of kisses going, across her chest, nuzzling my face into her shirt to find more skin. But then my kisses start to leave holes. Little holes, open and gaping and bleeding.

She keeps screaming. I'm no longer bathing but drowning. It is mindless pain and fear and screaming. I want to run away from her, the noise and the blood. Slow motion takes over my movements and the most I can get is a step. I can't push back any further.

I turn around, trying to see what's blocking me, but I'm surrounded by people. At every turn, a wall of them.

The oxygen is being sucked out of the dark place. My lungs constrict with the sharp, stabbing pain of being unable to breathe. My body trembles, my arm broken and dotted with bleeding crescents.

Screaming floods my ears. The more the crowd seems to push against me, the less air I seem to have, but the more I scream, too.

Then I see her. My ginger girl. My lips still feel wet from the kisses, my skin still tingles from where she touched me. She has been pulled away from me, but she is still in clear view. The bodies around her are black and shapeless. All that is clear is her face. Those eyes. That hair.

Blood starts to seep from every one of her orifices except her eyes. They take a steel-like grip on me. I stare back. It's not like I can do anything else. I feel my limbs get heavier, as though they aren't even mine. Hunks of meat, bleeding and screaming and tired and empty.

My ginger girl opens her mouth, shouting. But the voice sounds doesn't belong to her. It's muffled, coming from another memory. Gruff. Masculine. Full of hatred.

I scream and scream and scream until nothing is left of me apart from blood and noise and blackness and those green, green eyes.

4

I saw my bedroom. The curtains closed, but morning light filled the room, the dust dancing in the seeping rays.

Underneath me, the duvet rustled as I pulled it off the sweaty parts of my body. It had clung to parts of me that I hadn't even realised could get so sweaty. My muscles protested against my movements, feeling tight and tired. The casted arm felt dead, a hunk of hinderance attached to my elbow.

In the hospital, my bed was automated. At the push of a button, I could be in any position possible. Back home, I had to do all the work. Pushing myself upright one-handed still felt strangely alien. I clambered against myself until I was sitting up against the bed frame. I faced the curtained windows, wishing I had the energy to get up and open them, let the sun burst into the room. Instead, my sticky body stayed still. Trapped against its own capabilities and the heavy peach pit stuck in my stomach.

On my bedside table, my phone vibrated. I groaned, pushing myself a little too far so that I could reach it. Tugging, it unplugged itself from the charger, and I sloped back down. I clicked the wake button and scrolled through the notifications. So much of it was rubbish. Blah blah liked blah blahs photo.

I scrolled along until I found what I was looking for. His reply.

Nathan's name seemed brighter on the screen than any of the others. The weight in my stomach seemed to spark, catching fire with sparks of nervousness. The sparks didn't feel pleasant though. They didn't feel like butterflies or that kind of shaky happy anxiety you get when you're both nervous and excited. It just felt like shit.

But still, I opened the message.

hey! it's great to hear from u. how u doing? hows that arm? am i allowed to ask how you broke it yet? ;)

I cringed a little. I smiled a little. My better instincts inside me told me not to reply, that this couldn't go anywhere good. He didn't know the real Lucy. But the destructive ones made me reply.

No, you're not allowed to ask. But it does hurt. How are you feeling now you're sans appendix?

Exhaling, I realised I was still shaky. Maybe it was from messaging Nathan, or maybe the dream, or maybe getting myself up. All I knew was that everything felt a little too difficult. The day felt a little too hard to face. With a bit of effort, I got out of bed and started my morning routine. Shower, brush teeth, get dressed, eat breakfast. I'd never realised how monotonous the routine had become. I zoned out, completely. My head was empty of everything but worry. About Nathan, about Brittany, about anything other than Pride.

Whenever my head turned to that last one, it started screaming. Black and deafening and I had to scream over it to make it stop.

I went through it all. Letting my body do the showering and eating, while my mind cycled through worrying about different things. Everything buzzed around me, blurry movements that I couldn't remember after I'd done them. When I'd eaten my last bite of my overly-sugared Shreddies and washed my bowl, I felt jarred. The blurry motion stopped, and although I didn't feel exactly connected again, I felt less disconnected. My routine was over. The mandatory done.

I stared into the sink. I didn't know what to do now.

School wasn't to start for another few weeks and I had no idea what to do with that time. There was no point trying to get a summer job now, when summer was so nearly over. I could help my parents with the endless throwing away piles of memories into skips in preparation for moving, but I didn't want to. And it wasn't as if I could call Brittany up, say sorry and ask her to hang out.

Well, I mean, I could. Knowing Brittany, she wouldn't even need a sorry. She'd hear me say it, throw a playful punch (that surprisingly has a lot of power in it for someone so tiny) and tell me to shut up.

I knew it would be OK. If I just rang her. If I even texted. We'd been best friends for so long. We weren't strangers to the odd spat, disagreement, off days. And like after those other things, we'd say sorry and go back to the way we always were. Best friends.

With one hand clutching the cool metal of the sink and the other holding my phone, I hovered over her contact name. My thumb was so close to pressing her name, but I couldn't make myself actually touch it.

I stayed there, floating over her little icon on my phone. It was an old photo of the two of us, face-painted up for some charity fun run, looking ridiculous. For a second, the flicker of the memory motivated me, pushing me to call her, when Nathan's name appeared at the top of the screen.

He'd replied.

sans appendix? holy crap… well, i think i've figured out why u were in the hospital

Pride

My heart palpitated. I didn't care if I looked eager. I replied straight away, anxiety soaring through my veins.

Oh, yeah? Why?

…

cuz ur a giant nerd, obviously. no one uses the word "sans". ur parents took u to hospital to remove the nerdiness from ur brain ;)

If that was true, I wouldn't still be using the word "sans", would I?

…
true. i guess i need to go to hospital for being a giant idiot

I have to agree. :-P

…

lol

I kept watching my screen, seeing if he'd reply more than just an abbreviation, but the typing bubbles didn't come up again.

Maybe he was put off by the way I typed. Maybe I wasn't making the conversation interesting enough. Maybe he somehow secretly knew I was gay and someone had tried to kill me for that and he wouldn't have a chance with me and now he wasn't interested and…

this may be a bit forward but do u wanna meet up and go out somewhere? i need to get away from my parents for a bit, they will not stop fussing around me. that sans appendix life, ey? lol

My fingers hovered over the keyboard, seemingly unable to type anything the same way I hadn't been able to press Brittany's contact.

It did seem forward. Part of me wanted to delete the conversation, close Facebook and call Brittany. It's what Old Lucy would have done, for sure. Creepy person messages you online? Delete. Block. Erase.

But it wasn't as if I hadn't met Nathan. It wasn't as if, for our entire conversation, being forward seemed to be his style.

And it wasn't as if I had anything better to do that day, either.

And it wasn't as if the worst thing that could've happened me hadn't have already happened. I mean, sure, there were plenty of other crazy horrible things that could happen to me. My brain had started going into a whirring overdrive listing them all. But I'd lived through being shot at. It couldn't get that much worse.

Most of all though, I *really* didn't feel like being alone with my thoughts. So I said yes.

*

As it turned out, Nathan lived in Brighton. But thanks to living within the threshold of a London zone, the public transport was pretty good.

To make it fair, we decided to meet somewhere in the middle of where we both lived in a place called Crawley. I wasn't excited about going to Crawley, but I was heavily relieved to know I wouldn't have to go back to Brighton. Not yet, anyway. I couldn't face it.

It took us both just under an hour to get there. We met outside the station, awkwardly greeting each other, before deciding to head to whatever was the first cafe we came across.

Seeing him again was strange. It was only a few days ago now, but it felt a lifetime had passed. It felt like we'd never even met before. He'd become a figure synonymous with escape in my head, but seeing him made him feel real. It made me think about what I was doing for a second. That I could be hurting someone who was actually real, a human like me. Not some words and a pixelated picture of a guy holding a big fish.

"So, you been here before?" Nathan interrupted, walking alongside me.

I scoffed. "That sounds like such a movie line."

"Hey!" He replied with a faux indigence. "I'm just making conversation."

"I know, sorry," I said. I didn't know if it was OK to laugh. I was basing my assumptions on who he was based off one Facebook conversation and a very awkward encounter in the hospital. I didn't know his style of humour or if he was actually someone who was quite forward. Maybe he just liked me and was trying damn hard to get to know me.

I glanced over at him. Same dirty blonde hair, shining against the mid-August sun. Any other girl would fawn over the fact he was likely trying harder than any other guy in the history of guys.

But not me. And that fucking sucked. I fucking sucked.

I needed to tell him. I had to tell him I was gay, I couldn't do this, something felt wrong-

"But have you been here before?" he said, interrupting me again.

The heavy peach pit that was once in my stomach had made its way to my throat. So I swallowed, hard, before replying: "Yeah. Twice actually."

"You like it?"

"Uh, no," I said. "I mean, it's OK I guess. If you like… greyness and shopping and being bored."

Nathan laughed. Heartily. It reminded me that neither of us were exactly not feeling the awkward-anxious mood cloud over us. "OK, so what places *do* you like?" he asked.

Brighton, I thought immediately. I loved it there. I loved the coloured houses and the rickety, small lanes. I loved the long pier where you could see the sea beneath your feet; the flat boardwalk on the beach where you'd get sand in your socks. Brighton had always felt like a home away home for me. When my parents told me we were selling our home, the home I'd lived in since I was a baby, my world went into category ten hurricane mode. The only place I could ever see myself settling down again in, was Brighton.

I didn't know where else I liked. I'd never been abroad - we'd never been able to afford it. But it wasn't as if I could tell Nathan about how much I adored his city. He'd make me go there. And I couldn't do that. I knew that more than anything.

"Um, I went to the Lake District one year," I finally replied. "My parents and I stayed in a caravan. My grandparents came, too. It was nice there."

Nathan nodded. "Yeah, I've been there once on a school trip. It's nice."

At that point, we found a little cafe. It looked kind of run down; peeling paint and broken flower pots outside. But we stuck to our 'go to the first cafe we see' rule, and stepped inside.

It was quaint. I liked it. It may have been a little ram shackled, but it felt homely. The walls were painted a warm orange and there were books everywhere. There was something about being surrounded by books that made me feel at ease.

We sat down at a free table. There were only two other people here, but there were only four tables to choose from to begin with. By the size standards of the place, it was pretty busy.

"What do you want? I'll go order," Nathan offered.

"Uh God, anything that's cold would feel like heaven to be honest," I said, flapping my shirt to bring my hot body some breeze.

"Coming right up." Nathan smiled. It was the same bright, flashy one. One that would make a millions girls drop at his feet. One that would make Brittany drop her underwear. Man, if she met him, she would kill me for not showing him to her earlier…

Thinking of Brittany made the peach pit sink back into my stomach. I watched as he sauntered over to the counter, overhearing him order two Diet Cokes with ice.

He was physically attractive. That was for sure. He *looked* good. He was slim, but his arms and legs seemed strong with muscle. His hair was all wavy and poufy in the same way that all the guys from boybands were. His face was good, too.

It was all good. But I didn't feel anything for him. I'd never felt anything for any boy. I just *didn't*. I could tell, easily, if they were theoretically attractive or not. But it never went any deeper than that. I could never see myself kissing them, or touching them. I never got that in-your-heart feeling of lust and attraction and wanting.

I wished I did. I wish I'd been able to exchange secret crushes at sleepovers, instead of having a crush on one of the girls I was at the sleepover with. I wish I'd been able to get excited about discos and proms and dances, instead of worrying that if I didn't have a date then *everyone would find out!*

Sometimes, being gay fucking sucked. That was the truth of it. Being something that wasn't the cookie cutter mould, that everyone else seemed to fit into, was exhausting. My entire life has been fighting to just be able to feel like myself. And when I finally did try to be me - little lesbian Lucy, out and at Pride and enjoying life - it all fucked up.

I couldn't even be me. Everything felt stupidly fucking complicated. For once, I wished I could be the normal teenage girl. The one worried about getting the right grades for university. Not whether a gunman would burst into this cafe right now and shoot her for wanting to kiss girls. The one who would be excited about being at a cafe, on a first date with a cute boy.

I wanted to know what normality felt like.

"Two Diet Cokes!" Nathan proclaimed, pushing a glass bottle towards me.

Drips of the condensation on the glass wet my hand as I gulped down the drink. "Oh God, that's good," I sighed. The iciness spread through my chest and stomach, sending little goose bumps down my warm arms. The sensation didn't last long against the non-air conditioned cafe and heat of the August sun, so I ended up downing the rest of the drink.

"Someone was thirsty," Nathan said.

I shrugged. "It was nice and cold."

"Something to really…" Nathan sipped his drink, swilling the liquid around his mouth. "Ahh… savour."

"Shut up," I smiled. "I haven't had Diet Coke in forever. We always get the regular stuff."

"We?" Nathan asked.

I gripped the empty bottle, the reality, a little tighter. "Oh, yeah. Just a friend."

Nathan nodded, taking a sip from his bottle. It

never occurred to me beforehand how inseparable in my mind Brittany and I had truly become. I knew she was my best friend and that we did pretty much everything together, but this was the first time I'd noticed myself unconsciously saying the "we".

In a weird way, it was like we were a couple. When I first came out, people had asked us both a gazillion times a day if we had been secretly dating this entire time. The idea was so preposterous to us both that it never even bothered us. It didn't matter what people thought of us

"So, you're in sixth form, right?" Nathan asked.

"Yeah," I replied. "Are you?"

"Yep. Doing Maths, Physics and P.E."

I lifted my eyebrows up, impressed. "You must be stupidly clever."

"I'm really not," Nathan laughed. "I dunno. When I first chose P.E., it's 'cause I thought it'd be cheaper than going to the gym."

"And was it?"

"Well, turns out, A-Level P.E. is way less running about playing football than it was before."

I couldn't help but laugh. Something about talking to him put me at ease. It felt easy, but still with that right amount of awkward that happens at the start of a friendship. But there was still a rattling snake hissing at the pit of my stomach; anxious, anxious, anxious. Telling me he didn't think it was just friendship.

For the first time that day, the voice I'd heard the other day came back to me.

You could just go along with it.

With what, him thinking this isn't just friendship? I wondered. I couldn't do that. What would be the point? It was... weird.

It could just be for a bit.

...

To see what it feels like.

I had a good idea what it would feel like. Nothing. Because I'm gay. I wouldn't feel anything.

But you could feel normal.

…

Even for a second. You could be like a normal girl.

…

You could just be like everyone else. It could all be so much easier.

I guess…

You'd never have been shot at if you weren't gay.

…

You'd never have been at Pride.

…

The absence of you could have meant that someone else would've survived.

The ginger girl…

My eyes went black, then fired with orange hair and green eyes and red blood. And then I couldn't breathe.

Nathan waved his hand in front of my face. "Earth to Lucy, Earth to Lucy, are you receiving?" he said.

My heart constricted in my chest. "Y… Yes. Sorry."

"Don't be sorry," Nathan said, his voice light. "You OK?"

Normal. You could have normal. "Yes. I'm fine," I tried to make my voice sound like his. A moment of silence passed between us before I spoke again. "You know what? Let's go do something."

"Like what?"

"There's this adventure park thing a bus ride away from here," I start blabbering. My voice is fast, nervous. "You, like, climb up and around trees and it's really high and stuff. We could go. We could go right now."

"Won't it be busy?" Nathan asked. "And will they

even let you with your broken arm?"

I shrugged. "No idea. Let's find out."

Nathans' mouth spread into a cheek-to-cheek smile. "OK. Why not?"

So, we got on a bus and went there. I'd never wanted to go to this place before. I'd only even known about it because Brittany had tried to beg me into going on her 16th birthday. She was all for this thrill-seeking adrenaline stuff. But I, terrified of heights, was very much not all for it.

But that was old Lucy. New Lucy, the one who ignored the texts from her best friend and hung out with a strange boy, would love this. She would have to.

When we got to the adventure place, we waited for half an hour because of the summer holidays busy rush. We sat in the little cafe next door, waiting for our hour to come up, drinking more Diet Cokes and chatting. We talked about our plans for after school. How I was planning on applying to university to do English or something, but wasn't sure. He talked about how he secretly always wanted to be an astronaut and that's the only reason he was taking Maths and Physics at school.

When we were called out by one of the employees for our turn, we had to wait an extra half an hour. Their manager had to go over their company policy and rules because of my broken arm. They almost didn't let me do it, but eventually they agreed, making me state I knew I was at risk, etc. etc. That, and I'd have to have a spotter on the ground watching me at all times.

"Are you *sure* this is OK? 'Cause we can go again when your arm isn't... you know, broken." Nathan asked.

"No," I insisted. "I really want to do this."

Afterwards, I faced my fears on the treetops course. I screamed a lot but Nathan kept making me laugh. We took way longer than we should have because of my arm, but it was OK. Nathan stood at the end of each one, encouraging me. Occasionally making fun of me for being such a chicken. It was weird, doing something I'd been so scared of, only to find out that it was kind of fun. Even if I was shaking with adrenaline afterwards.

No one gave us any weird stares. No one even gave us a second glance. That was the first sense of normality that I felt. Being able to hang out with someone, have fun and laugh… and have no one care. No one look at you because you were two girls, touching gently, touching too much to be just friends.

I went home that night with a smile on my face. The minute I walked through the door to see the packing boxes and missed texts from Brittany, I felt heavy again. So I arranged to meet up with Nathan again the next day.

And it kept going like that. For the next two weeks, we became inseparable. I would leave the house at midday and come back when it got dark. The nightmares stopped. I was so exhausted most of the time from wandering about everywhere and anywhere with Nathan that I fell asleep in seconds. I even started to look forward to waking up.

I barely texted Brittany. I didn't see her once. My parents caught on almost immediately. It was odd for Brittany and I not to hang out in the same way Nathan and I were. Kind of wrong. They even started getting worried about me and what I was doing with this guy they'd never met.

One night, over dinner, my Mum demanded that she and Dad wanted to meet Nathan. "We just want to know what he's like!" Mum said.

"You've been spending pretty much every second with him since you got back," My Dad noted, shovelling some mash potato into his mouth.

I twirled the food around on my plate. "I know. But he's nice, I promise. I mean, I wouldn't be spending all my time with him otherwise."

My Mum smiled. I guess to her, at this point, I was seeming OK. I wasn't screaming at night anymore or shouting at them if they even looked at me. I wasn't the cranky Lucy they'd met after what happened at Pride. The fact I was ignoring Brittany's constant texts and visits was and was worthy of concern. Especially now I was hanging out with someone they'd never heard of until five minutes ago.

"We know, Lucy," My Mum said. "And we trust you. But we would like to meet him."

"And you've been a lot happier lately," Dad commented. "And after everything that… happened to you… we… we'd like to thank him for making you feel a bit better, I guess."

My parents looked at me, doe-eyed and soft.

Nathan was one of the only people who didn't look at me like I was a victim. I was fully aware it was because he didn't know anything about what happened to me, but it was refreshing. Everything about Nathan felt refreshing. He didn't know Lucy. I could be anyone with him. I could be normal.

I wasn't thrilled about the idea of my fake-normality world meeting my actual real world. It kind of terrified me, thinking how it could all could get ruined. Not only could Nathan find out I'd lied him about pretty much everything, but it could ruin whatever goodness I felt around him.

But I didn't have much of a choice. My parents hadn't ever stopped me from going out and doing stuff with friends and I wanted to keep it that way.

"Fine. You guys can meet him," I said. "I'll see if he's free for dinner tomorrow night."

My Mum smiled, and my Dad heaped another forkful of mashed potatoes into his mouth.

I kept swirling the food around on my plate.

5

It became an unspoken rule that the news wasn't allowed on the TV.

Every day, there was more coverage of the shooting. Victims names got leaked. Sobbing families got interviewed. Politicians saying how awful and bad it all was. One day, I came downstairs and the TV was showing phone camera footage of the attack. I only had to hear the screams for my vision to go black and swallow me whole.

I'd lain on the floor, hands clutched at my head, howled for it to go away. Even after it had stopped, I could still hear it. Echoing and in line with my heart beat, scream after scream. My parents had to coax me, telling me over and over that it was off, I was OK.

"Lucy, what happened?" My Mum had begged.

I forced myself to sit up at that point. So far, for the few weeks I'd been home, I'd managed to keep it all secret. The nightmares, the flashbacks, the feelings. I'd tucked them away inside me, hidden them behind my layers of flesh. When I hung out with Nathan and things started to ease up, I thought it was going to go away. But moments like that reminded me all I was doing was putting a plaster over a broken bone.

"Nothing," I said, meek and quiet, my voice hoarse. Maybe I'd been screaming too. I didn't know.

"Lucy," My Mum repeated, her voice in that calm but firm way that somehow only mothers can pull off. "Talk to us."

"We're your parents and we're worried about you," My Dad went on. "You've been disappearing everyday and you've fallen out with Brittany and now this…"

"I haven't fallen out with Brittany," I said on instinct, even though I knew that wasn't really true. It had been a week since I'd replied to any message she'd tried to send. It was too hard. Everything was:

hey, r u busy today?
   ...
hellloooooo???
   ...
??? wondering where the fuck my best friend has gone
   ...
wanna hang out?
   ...
lucy? what's wrong? why aren't you talking to me? x
   ...
lucy, i love u. ur my best friend. i duno why ur not replying but i miss u a lot and im really fucking worried. please just reply.
   ...
ok then

All of which were too hard to reply to.

Truth was, when I thought about Brittany, I thought about Pride. How I'd almost killed my best friend. How, in some way, I'd killed other people who weren't my best friend but were someone else's best friend. I know that I didn't hold the gun, but if I wasn't there, I'd have made space for someone to run away. For someone to hide. For someone to survive. But the only way I wouldn't have been there is if I wasn't gay. That's what it all came down to, really.

Somewhere deep down, I knew it didn't make sense.

But after replaying someone's death in my head a thousand times over, I was convinced. And because of all that, I didn't know how to hang out with Brittany. I didn't even know how to talk to her.

My Mum shook her head at me. Neither of my parents were of the confrontational style. This was out of their depth. They were swimming around, hopeless to find the finishing line.

"Are you OK, now?" My Dad asked, breaking the silence that had fallen over us.

I nodded, my arms holding me up even though they felt wafer-thin.

"Let me get you some tea," he said, hauling himself up before heading toward the kitchen.

Mum sighed, deep and full. "Come on, love," she stood up, too, and held out her hand for me. I grabbed onto it, relishing the steadiness. "Why don't you start running a nice bath, I'll bring you your tea."

"OK," I agreed, even though I wasn't a fan of baths. They had always made me feel sleepy and a little headache-y. But I had to try to pretend to be OK, despite what happened.

When I was about to turn away, she pulled me in for a hug. She rubbed my back, stroked my hair. Whispered in my ear that it was going to be OK. That it was horrible but I was safe now.

But, trapped in her arms, all I felt was suffocated. My mind went back to being stuck in that crowd, unable to breathe. Squished so tight you couldn't make your lungs expand even a quarter of the way. I felt my body go cold, remembering.

As quickly as the hug had begun, it ended. Mum walked to the kitchen, leaving me there. Standing, warm and breathing, but not really.

My fingers find their ways back to the crescent

moons. They've long since scabbed over, but it didn't take much force to make them bleed once more.

*

"What're we having for dinner tonight? Nathans' text me and asked."

"Fish, obviously," Mum said. "You said he liked fish."

"I don't know if he likes fish. I just know he likes fishing," I said, remembering telling her about one of his fishing escapades. He had gone out with his Dad one day and hooked onto something huge in the lake. It was so big and heavy it ended up capsizing their boat. They never found out what it was. To this day, Nathan and his Dad pretend it was the Loch Ness Monster. Despite the fact they live as far away from Scotland as possible.

"Well, fishermen probably like fish," Mum replied. "And if they don't, what are they fishing for?"

I smiled. My stomach was tight and full of knots. Ironically, it felt like someone was fishing in there. I didn't know what expect out of tonight. It had felt like I was twelve years old with my first boyfriend, annoyed and anxious that my embarrassing parents were demanding to meet him.

Part of me liked that feeling. It was never something I'd gotten to experience. I knew that not actually that many people had that happen to them when they were twelve. Life wasn't like the movies, after all. But it was nice to pretend, for a little while, that life was like the movies and I was a normal girl.

It had been hard making the dinner work. Our house move was going very slowly, but my parents were going very quickly. Despite that it would be a month or two until we could leave, so much of our stuff was either packed or thrown away. The sale was going slowly. Problems with stuff I didn't understand. Mortgage applications and finances and buyers and estate agents… When I tried to ask to find out more about it all, my Mum goes off in a flurry about this and that and other stuff. I don't care to listen too much about it. Whatever kept me in our home for longer, I'm a fan of. Even if it gets Mum all twirly and means we don't have as many dishes for dinner.

"He's going to think we're people who live out of boxes or something," My Mum fretted, setting out mismatching plates onto the table.

"Oh no," I say, sarcasm dripping from my lips. "Not people who live out of boxes or something!"

"Hush, you," Mum says, faux-scolding me by pretending to whack my hand with a plate. "I want him to think good of us. Like you clearly think of him."

I looked down at the plate she put in front of me; rounded and a deep maroon red. It reminded me of blood. Whenever either of my parents mentioned Nathan, the uninvited voice in my head filled in the gaps of any unsaid words.

If you were normal…

You mean, if I were straight?

Same thing, right?

I…

If you were normal, your parents would be implying so much more right now.

Like what?

Listen. You "clearly think good of him". But that's all you think of him.

So?

Any other parent, one to a normal little girl, would be teasing them about this boy they so clearly had a crush on. It would be all oohs and aahs and when are we going to meet his parents…

God, I hated that voice. I hated how it made so much sense, and yet none at all. And how I believed every single lie it told me.

Delicious smells of cooking filled the room. I sat, breathing in the lemon marinade scent in the air, and watched my parents cook from the archway. They always seemed most in love when they're cooking together. Acting as though it's a choreographed dance routine, they chopped and peeled, sautéed and stirred, twisting around each other. Between verses of re-oiling the pan and washing up the chopping boards, they found snippets of time to steal a kiss. It was absorbing and fulfilling. The house we were moving to had a very small kitchen. I didn't know how they could even say yes to it and give this up.

"What time is he getting here?" My Mum asked.

"Uh," I started. "You have mashed potato on your cheek. And soon. He said his train was getting in at half past."

Mum checked her electronic watch. She always wore it. It was one of those things where they tell you how many steps you'd done and what your heart rate was at. I had no idea why, but she just loved to sometimes announce how fast her heart was going at a particular moment. "Oh, bugger. I better get dressed." she said. She kissed my Dad on the cheek. "You're OK to look after the potatoes while I nip upstairs?"

"Yes, dear, I think I can manage it," Dad joked back before pulling her in for a proper kiss. They were so smoosh-y sometimes.

My Mum flounced up the stairs like a lovesick schoolgirl. I tucked my chin into the crook of elbow and wondered if I'd ever find something like what they have together.

For a second, I tried to imagine what it would be like if I tried to keep things going with Nathan. What exactly did I expect was going to happen? That, eventually, maybe one day I'd feel the same way about him as he does about me? That we'd kiss and make love and get married and dance around the kitchen like my parents?

The whole idea felt preposterous. Stupid, even. All of a sudden, I had no idea how I'd ever thought about stringing this boy along for my own gratification. It felt so wrong. There was no way it could end in anything other than hurt. That was clear to me now.

And sure, we'd seen each other a lot. But neither of us had ever called it a *date*. We'd never held hands. He'd never tried to kiss me. We sometimes hugged before saying goodbye, but it was friendship-y. Right? I was sure of it. Possibly. Maybe.

Either way, it hadn't gone too far yet. I could still pull it off as just friends. Maybe I'd even come clean to him about the whole thing. I'd have to. I could pretend I was afraid of telling him, but considering we were such good *friends*, I felt as though I could trust him...

At that moment, the doorbell rang, echoing through the house.

"Get the door, Lucy, will you, love?" Dad asked, stirring gravy.

Anxiety fluttered through my stomach. My thoughts flew through my head, going a hundred miles per hour. I knew I'd have to put out some serious friend zone vibes tonight, somehow...

I opened the door, and there stood Nathan. The smell of his sweet yet strong cologne hit me. The manly scent unpleasantly mingling with the lemon from the kitchen. He was wearing smart black trousers and a proper looking shirt.

The amount of effort he'd put into his outfit was too much, and way too formal for dinner with my parents. But what stood out were the bouquet of flowers he was holding out toward me. Multi-coloured tulips. I remember walking by a flower stand and telling him that they were my favourite. I couldn't believe he had remembered.

In that moment, I knew it was too late. He thought we were more than friends. He thought there was *something* between us. I tried to tell myself that maybe the flowers were for my Mum or something. Or a thanks for inviting me to dinner present. But it was useless. He handed them over to me and gave me that big, beaming smile. The kind of smile that said 'oh wow, I can't believe the girl I like has invited me to meet her parents'.

"Hey, Lucy," Nathan said, a softness to his voice. "Do... do you like them?"

His nervousness was slightly endearing. He was always so oddly confident for a teenage boy. But this, a clear step up in whatever we were to him, was breaking his confident exterior.

"Yeah, thank you, I love them. Uh... I'll just... put them here. Thank you." I stammered, taking the bouquet, hovering around for a place for them to go before settling on the side of the bannister. "Come in."

He stepped through the doorway and into the hallway. He looked so large and protruding against the familiar surroundings. One life meeting another.

"You've such a lovely home," Nathan said.

"Yeah," I agreed. "I don't want to move out of it."

"You're moving house? You didn't tell me that!"

Yeah, cause I don't tell you anything real, I thought. "Sorry," I shrugged. "It's been so hectic."

"I can get that," Nathan said. I thought for a second

that he was utterly forgiving, until I realised he didn't know in any way that I was lying. Why wouldn't he be forgiving? Why would he think that I was anything other than someone whose house move was so hectic it kind of... slipped her mind?

I was such a fucking awful person.

"Come in," I muttered before heading toward the kitchen.

My Dad, in a very messy apron, was still hunched over the cooker. He was shaking out his signature pepper and paprika mix into the potatoes.

"Dad?" I asked, tapping his shoulder.

He jumped slightly. "Oh! Hey! I'm Lucy's Dad!" He stuck out his hand. It was messy from cooking, but Nathan still politely shook it anyway.

"I'm Nathan. It's nice to meet you."

"Sandra! Lucy's Nathan is here!" My Dad yelled up. Their bedroom was right above the kitchen. Because of that, it was always ridiculously warm inside their room. Mum used to say she loved it because it made her save money on the heating bills. When we started the whole moving house process, she changed her mind and said she hated it because it made all her clothes smell like cooking. I didn't see the problem with that. Especially with the delicious dishes they make.

"Need us to take anything through, Mr. Brown?" Nathan asked. The difference in his confidence was palpable. He almost felt as if he was a different person. So much more awkward and shy and try hard-y. I tried to suppress a little giggle at his efforts, which led him to shoot me a faux-evil glare.

My Dad smiled at him. My parents were easy to please. If you were polite, they'd love you. "Please, call me Phil. Names Phillip, but I like you, so you can call me Phil," he joked. Nathan made a little, unsure laugh back.

"You can take the gravy to the table, if you like. Lucy, get the fish. It's sitting in the microwave to keep it warm while I finish up this mash."

"Lucy told you I like fish, eh?" Nathan asked, picking up the gravy boat.

"She sure did," Dad answered as he started on creaming the potatoes. "She said you liked actually going and fishing them, too."

I wrestled the baking dish with the fish out of the microwave. Lord knows how they managed to fit in there. It was massive. And heavy. And very difficult to do one-handedly. Fucking broken arm.

"I do! I love fishing," Nathan said. "You ever been?"

"No, I haven't actually. I'd bloody love to one day though."

"You should! It's fantastic. Really relaxing, which you wouldn't expect-"

It was weird, watching them get on so well. It all felt so normal and natural. I tried to imagine what it would be like if I'd brought a girl home for dinner instead. I didn't know if my Dad would be being this easy-going. I didn't know anything.

"Nathan, come on, I don't wanna drop this thing!" I said, my voice raised. My one good arm, taking most the weight of the baking dish, was beginning to keel in.

"Oooo-ooo-ooooh," My Dad mocked. "Someone's getting bossy."

"Shut up," I groaned.

"Are you alright with that?" Nathan asked, his voice gentle. "I can take it, if you want."

"No. It's fine. I can do it." I said, a little snappy. I hated being pandered to. My arm was broken. I wasn't dying.

Not like all those others around you. Dying. Screaming.

Remember?

Shut up!

Nathan followed me through the arch into our dimly-lit dining room. It used to be full of odd paintings my Mum had collected over the years at various artsy cafes. She'd always wanted to be seen as someone with style and taste. To me, it had always looked like the world's worst craft fair. But now it was gone, and the walls were bare, it made everything feel empty. I wouldn't even get to see them all again in the new houses' dining room. Mum had thrown away so many of them, vowing not to fill the new house with clutter.

We placed the dishes down on the table, with me putting the fish in the centre. It looked amazing. Grilled salmon with lemon and thyme and rosemary… My mouth would've normally salivated at the smell of it, but I felt sick. My stomach twisted with nerves. Nathan was actually here. This was actually happening. He'd brought me flowers and joked with my Dad. They wanted to meet him to make sure he wasn't some 25 year old drug dealer taking advantage of my current vulnerability. Nathan just thought he'd met a cute girl who he'd been out with a lot recently and was now meeting her parents.

It all felt so fucked up. In that moment, all I wanted to do was run. Run away from it all. I didn't know how to undo the knot I'd tied. If I ran away, then maybe someone else could untie it.

But my feet wouldn't move. They wouldn't run away or listen to me at all. Instead, they copied Nathan's movements. Stepping back to pull out a chair. Stepping forward to sit in the chair. Pushing yourself in toward the table.

I felt my body shaking. Sweat bunched up my fringe. I started to feel anxious about the fact I was feeling anxious. I didn't want my parents to worry, or for Nathan to ask questions. I wanted to be normal Lucy. Normal fucking Lucy.

So I did what I knew would ground me. What always seemed to work. My hand burrowed its way into my shirt sleeve. They were long-sleeves, and it was boiling hot, but it'd be visible otherwise. My fingernails found the crescent-moon shapes and dug in. Hard. I kept on clinging, harder and harder, until all I could focus on was the pain. It only took a few seconds. Even though I knew what I was doing was unhealthy, was dangerous, it made me feel strong somehow. Like I could overcome anything.

When I stopped, I excused myself to go to the bathroom so I could quell the bleeding. People asking questions about the blood on my sleeve was a big giveaway that I didn't want. I'd done this whole routine a couple times. Anxious, hurt myself, bleed, bathroom. Anxious, hurt myself, bleed, bathroom. The fact that this horrible little coping method had become a routine was scary.

As I held pressure on the gouges with a piece of loo roll, I vowed that this would be the last time. Someone would find out what I was doing if I kept doing it. It wasn't healthy. I didn't want people to worry. There were a whole plethora of reasons for me to stop doing it. But the minute I left that bathroom behind me and heard the laughter downstairs, I knew it wouldn't be the last time.

When I got back to the dining room, my Mum had joined us. She looked ever so pretty in her make-up and smart shirts, always the one to try to make a great first impression.

"Oh, Lucy! We've just been chatting to Nathan about the time you guys went to that tree-top adventure course." Mum said, raising her eyebrows at me.

"Yeah. I put on my big girl brave boots."

"You sure did!" she said, laughing. "You know, Nathan, she's *always* had a fear of heights. Even when she was just a toddler. I couldn't park anywhere other than the ground floor in car parks without her screaming her head off!"

Nathan laughed along with her. I felt like screaming my head off.

"Dad, is the mash done?" I called.

"Sure is." He came through the archway, carrying a pot of creamy looking mashed potatoes. He popped back into the kitchen one last time to fetch the peas and the carrots before sitting down in his usual seat next to Mum.

"Right!" Mum proclaimed. "Let's dig in."

Things were quiet for a bit while we all served up what we wanted and started to eat. I tried to make the amount on my plate look normal, but it was hard. Serving myself what would be considered a normal portion of food isn't something I'd struggled with before Pride. But since it, I'd lost my appetite. I hadn't felt hungry even once. I had to remind myself to eat so that questions wouldn't be asked and eyebrows wouldn't be raised. I was skinnier than I'd ever been in my life. If Brittany could see me, I couldn't imagine the copious amounts of food she'd try and shove down me.

"This is beautiful, Sandra," Nathan told her.

Mum swallowed. "Thank you! It was no bother, really."

"I'd love to be able to cook like this," Nathan said.

"Oh! Well, I'm sure we could have a cooking day altogether when we've moved?" Mum offered. "It would be nice to get Lucy in the kitchen for once!"

I rolled my eyes. "I'm rubbish at cooking."

"That's 'cause you never do it," Dad interjected. A snicker went around the table before we all started to eat again.

"So, when are you moving?" Nathan started.

"Oh, God, uh," Mum said, looking over at Dad. They both smiled broadly at each other, an mutually exasperated expression flying across their faces. "It's hard to say."

"We're expecting for it all to be done and ready by January at the very latest."

"Oh," Nathan paused. "What's making it take so long? I mean, is that even long? I've never moved house before."

"It's not uncommon for these things to get delayed a lot," Dad explained. "We're having a bit of trouble with the buyers of this house. Their mortgage applications got flagged up by the bank. We're pretty sure it's going to be OK but it means we have to wait until we can close the deal on our new house."

"Bit annoying, but worth the wait!" Mum chirped.

I scooped a pile of peas into my mouth and tried to make myself focus on chewing them. All I wanted to do was reach into my sleeve again, but I knew I couldn't. There was no inconspicuous way of doing it when everyone was eating at the dinner table. I made myself keep putting food into my mouth. Focusing on my teeth ripping apart the fish's flesh and trying not to think of bullets going through chests and heads and stomachs.

Somehow, I got through dinner without having my nails rip into my own flesh again. Nathan and I offered to help with the washing up. It was something my Mum would ordinarily latch onto the idea of. But as Nathan was a first-time guest in the Brown household, we got let off the hook.

I hadn't planned for what Nathan and I would do after dinner, so I took him up to my room with the idea of showing him around. The rest of the house had been severely packed-up, but I'd done the bare minimum with my room. I didn't see the point of even trying to pack up anymore, especially now it was going to be sometime in January we'd move. I wanted to have *my* bedroom up until then, for as long as I could. Not just a bed sitting in a room.

We clambered up the stairs, bellies full and ripping. I stroked the walls of the hallway until we reached my door. The paint was soft, but chipping, and my heart ached. I couldn't hug a house goodbye and it hurt.

"This is my room," I announced as I opened the door.

Nathan was quiet as he stepped into the threshold. Everything in here screamed Lucy, but I guess he didn't know the real me enough to see that. He walked around, touching little items as he went along. He paused at the ballerina music-box on my bookshelf. It was the very first birthday present Brittany had ever gotten me. I knew her parents had probably bought it without any help or consultation from Brittany herself, but I still loved it. I still would keep it forever.

He looked at the books that weren't packed yet. Well-read copies of *Jane Eyre* and an embarrassing amount of young adult fantasy books. He walked over to my Everything Desk. I called it that because my whole life went on at that desk. I got ready there, I did my homework there, I read my books there… you name it. Surrounded on the wall by the Everything Desk was thumb-tacked photos of Brittany and I.

"Is this your friend?" he asked, gently.

I'd mentioned Brittany to him a number of times. Always just calling her 'my friend'. It was impossible to avoid her coming up in conversations. So many of my good stories or experiences had her in.

"Yeah, that's her. Her name's Brittany." I said, figuring that I wouldn't be able to keep it secret forever.

"Is she your best friend?"

"Yeah." I said softly.

"I'd love to meet her one day," Nathan said, turning back around to face me. "And I know my friends definitely want to meet you."

Now we were alone, confident Nathan was slipping through his polite mask. The big, broad smile he always seemed to wear around me had come back entirely and lighting up the entire room.

"Yeah," I said, again. I didn't know what else to say to him. Or to that. I didn't want Brittany to meet him. I didn't want to meet his friends. It was bad enough he'd met my parents, making what I was doing that bit extra real. I didn't want it to be real. All I'd wanted was to feel normal.

Dinner with my parents and Nathan was supposed to be normal. Everyone getting along and laughing and being friendly. I wanted it to be that easy for me to feel normality. I wanted to be able to bring a boy home. To have my father have male-banter with him. To have my straight Mum make comments about how handsome he was.

I wanted to pretend it could be like that. That it wouldn't be my Dad, his heart in the right place, not wanting to make any offensive judgements or comments, but making it awkward anyway. I didn't want it to be my Mum, saying I'd met a really beautiful girl, but knowing deep-down she didn't *actually* get it.

I loved my parents. They were accepting. They were great. But I doubted that they could ever make me feel 'normal'.

Looking at Nathan, I felt a chance for normal. He

got on with my parents. He was, objectively, pretty good looking. He was kind and funny and he liked me. Maybe, if I tried to make myself, I could like him too.

So, that night, when we put a movie on my laptop and sat down on my bed to watch it together, I didn't take away my hand when he held it. I didn't freeze up when he kissed my cheek goodbye.

After he left, I crawled into bed and I realised that right now was the safest I'd felt. Sure, I was keeping everything a secret from pretty much everyone. But now I knew that the man in my dreams wouldn't shoot me anymore. Not while I was being kissed by a boy.

6

I spent the entire next week in bed.

My parents fretted about me. Constantly. They bring me tea and toast, thinking that maybe I'd caught some sort of bug. Nathan texts and asks if I want to meet up. I use the excuse that I've got a lot of back to school summer homework that I need to catch up on. He's sympathetic and hopes to see me soon. Brittany doesn't text. At all.

And I laid. I laid there while the sun comes up. I laid while it goes back down. I ate bites of foods and sips of water. I don't shower. I barely sleep. I let a heavy sadness consume me.

It started in my stomach the second I closed the door to Nathan after dinner. It grew, spreading through my limbs. My blood got replaced with lead and my limbs couldn't seem to function anymore. I tried to read my favourite book. I tried to stream my favourite TV show. But nothing lifted it.

I knew I couldn't lay here forever. My parents would take me to a doctor who would ask me what's wrong and I'd turn into a melted puddle on the floor. I had to shake the heaviness off me, but it felt impossible. Sadness had started to eat me up.

When the first day of the new school year rolled around, I had no other choice but to get up. I was starting Year 13. We would be doing our applications to university. I was to supposed to have written a draft of my personal statement and decided on my top five

Pride

universities. I hadn't even picked what subject I wanted to study yet.

Pulling myself out of bed seemed like the most difficult thing I'd had to do in a long while. It was something that should've taken mere seconds but instead took minutes.

My legs wobbled underneath the weight of my body. I was lighter than I'd ever been before, but I had barely moved in days and it felt odd to have so much on me. With my eyes scrunched up, I walked over to my window and pulled open the curtains. It was still deliciously warm outside by the looks of things. The trees hadn't even started shedding their leaves in preparation for autumn yet.

All I wanted to do was curl into a ball on my window seat. I'd wrap my blanket around me and I'd stay there until the trees started to turn orange and brown.

But I knew I couldn't. I had to shower. And eat breakfast. And get my bag ready. And brush my hair. Oh God. Brushing my hair.

My brain thought of all the things I had to do and tried to do them, little by little. Walked to the bathroom. Grab a towel. Get in the shower. Wash. Get out the shower…

Somewhere along the way, my body just started to do these things. My limbs still felt heavy and unmoving, but they were doing it. I wasn't even thinking. I didn't feel as though I was the one controlling my body whatsoever. My body did everything while my brain wandered off, blurry and dozing and stuck in the in-between.

I stayed in this hazy, switched-off sense of reality until Mum kissed my head.

"Good luck at school today," she wished me. I thanked her, mouth full of soggy Cheerios I didn't realise I'd been chewing. "Your Dad will give you a ride if you want."

I swallowed, the disgusting lump sliding down my throat. My stomach twisted, rejecting the food. "That would be good, thanks," I replied. "See ya later."

Normally, Brittany would give me a ride. She'd passed her driving test only a couple months after turning 17. She bought a ram shackled banger of a car from eBay, which took all her savings. She babysat for her neighbours once in a blue moon and had been saving up for years, but she loved the old thing. I loved it, too, because it mean she could drive us both to McDonalds at 2am when we both couldn't sleep.

But since it had been a couple weeks with zero contact, I didn't think she'd come rolling up in the Volvo outside my house. She hadn't messaged me at all for a couple weeks now. The idea of Brittany ignoring me was frightening, even though that was exactly what I'd been doing to her.

You're an awful friend.

I know.

I threw away the rest of the mushy Cheerios before getting my Dad to give me a lift. I clambered into the car and tucked my knees up to my chin. The journey was only five minutes, but I settled into the seat, facing the window as it was five hours.

I thought about the little voice in the back of my head. It used to be a strange, unfriendly visitor that only came to me when things got a little much. But I'd been talking to it this entire week. It was almost as if I could summon it to me. The voice was still as unfriendly as ever, whispering mean things to me, as if it was a little devil sitting on my shoulder. But I respected that it always told me the truth. And I liked that I could just be honest with it, too. There was no hiding from the devil.

Pride

"You feeling ready for your last year of school, Luce?"

"Mmm," I murmured back.

"Nervous?"

"I guess."

My Dad paused for a second. "Have you been thinking about what happened to you?"

It felt like the car stopped. I kept waiting for my body to jolt forward and smash through the window screen, but it didn't happen.

My voice was small when I found it again. "Yes."

Dad was quiet. "I understand."

No, he doesn't.

...

He never will.

I know.

"I never said how sorry I am."

I furrowed my brows, but still stared out the window. "Why are you sorry?" I asked.

"I... I don't know, I'm sorry it happened, I guess," he explained. "You didn't deserve that."

"What, and the others did?" I snapped. I pictured the faces that I could remember from that day. They were blurry and fast moving like the trees outside the car window. They were all dead in my memories.

My Dad inhaled sharply. "No!" he exclaimed, indigent. "No... That's not what I meant at all."

"Yeah. I know. Sorry."

I heard him sigh. A little bit of guilt pumped out of me with my heartbeat. A little bit of annoyance pumped back in.

After two long minutes, we finally arrived at school. My Dad said goodbye and love you, and I said nothing. I felt unreasonably frosty. I didn't want to be here. I longed for my body to be sent back in the auto-pilot mode that

I'd managed to switch it to this morning.

I'd been to this same school for three years in a row. This would be my fourth and final. I knew every nook and cranny that this place had to offer. The secret make-out spots (that I'd never used). The holes in the fences you can sneak out of (that, if my parents ask, I'd never used either).

Brittany wasn't in many of my classes because she chose the more difficult A-Levels our school had. Contrary to what people thought of her, she was a brain-box. I'd always been semi-jealous of her for it. She could party all weekend and flunk out on her homework, but will still get A*s in every exam.

"I'd *never* go to Oxford or Cambridge though," she had said to me once after getting back some of our mock grades. "It's too pretentious. The parties would be absolute trash."

"You never know," I'd said back. "You're clever and you party. There will be other people like you."

"Pfft. Yeah, right," she'd scoffed. "Besides, I want to be the best. If I go to a university where everyone is already amazing, how will I ever get to top them all?"

I'd grinned back at her. I had loved seeing this side of Brittany. To her other friends, she put on such a cool, tough girl look. Fishnet tights, piercings, make-up to the heavens despite the school rules. And to top it off, a bewitchingly infectious smile. People loved Brittany. She knew how to let her hair down and be loose and fun. I was the complete opposite. I was kinda uptight, hated house parties and didn't really have that many friends outside of her. I guess to her, when she was with me, she felt allowed to be who she was underneath all that loud. She could be the hard-working, sweet and generous girl she always was, but never let free.

Pride

Walking through the hallways to my locker, I knew I'd have to face her today. Normally, I'd be pretty excited for the start of school. While Brittany took Maths, Physics and Computing, I took English Literature, Film Studies and Geography. I was always stuck in either the Arts or Humanities department while Brittany was constantly in the Science department. Even when we were best friends, tighter than a curls coil, I was happy with the arrangement. I adored my classes and I adored getting to hang out with Brittany on frees and at lunch.

But now I didn't know what was going to happen to us. It had been weeks without us speaking. In all the years of our friendship, we had never gone for longer than a week without talking. And that week was because Brittany had to spend a week in a caravan in the Lake District with her grandparents. When she came back, she slept over at my house for three whole days. "I genuinely thought I was going to fucking spontaneously combust from boredom, Lucy." she had said.

I smiled. Sweet memories of our friendship flitted through my head. In that moment, I felt as though I missed her. That I'd been so stupid these past few weeks. She was my best friend. I could talk to her about anything.

As I walked, I pulled my phone out of my pocket to send her a text. I didn't know what it would say, probably just I'm sorry, can we hang out and talk, or something. What stopped me was a text from Nathan that popped up on my screen the minute I unlocked the phone.

hey! i hope u have a good day at school today. x

He'd put an x.
A kiss. A fucking kiss.
I shoved the phone back in my pocket.

No. I had to reply. I couldn't just… ignore it. He would be upset. He would be confused.

Thanks. I hope you have a good day, too. x

My stomach twisted. It felt full and bloated and nauseous. I felt the taste of the soggy cereal in my mouth. How could one little letter feel like it meant so much? We'd never put kisses on the ends of our messages before.
Well, he did hold your hand.
…
And kiss your cheek.
…
It's pretty normal.
…
Not that you'd know anything about that.
…

I reached my locker. I was glad for the distraction of putting in the numbers to unlock it. 14-05. My birthday.

We'd had to empty them before we broke up for summer so that they could get cleaned. I'd had the same one for my entire time here now. Usually, when I got back to after such a long time, it felt kind of familiar. The little dents and strange stains that never came out. But looking at it now just felt cold. It looked the same as everyone else's. There was nothing special or different about it. It was a locker. I'd romanticised a locker. Tried to make it mine. I was pathetic.

I took books out of my backpack and shoved them into the space. I didn't realise how harshly I was putting them in until a pair of boys walked by me.

"What's that locker ever done to you, eh, blondie?"

"Period on the first day of school? Must be rough!"

I rolled my eyes, which made them cackle more.

They walked off down the corridor, loud and annoying.

I hated boys. I was so glad I was a lesbian.

No.

What?

Don't.

Don't what?

Don't try to make it OK.

Try to make what OK?

Your sexuality. Don't you remember what he said? What he shouted at you?

...

Faggots... Scum... Unnatural... Degenerates... Queers...

Leave me alone. Please.

Then behave. You have Nathan now. You can't think things like that. I'm just looking out for you, Lucy.

I guess...

I closed my locker door, trying not to hear the little voice in the back of my head. I felt like a fucking crazy person, having something talk to me like that. I was sure it wasn't the same thing as 'hearing voices'. Having an inner monologue was pretty normal, I figured. Even if you kind of talked to it.

I didn't get very far down the corridor when I felt a light tugging on my shoulder. I turned around to see Brittany.

She looked as Brittany as ever. Full of school uniform violations. A little tanned. Full of freckles. Her dyed black hair looked glossy. She must've recently had it re-done. The thought of that made my heart ping a little. I'd always been the one who dyed her hair for her. We'd sit in my bathroom, in the tub, getting black everywhere. Mum went mad the first time we did it and ruined the shower curtain. After that, she made us put up that curtain whenever we'd wanted to do it.

"Hey, you," she said.

Her voice was soft. Gentle. As if it was scared to hurt me. I wondered, for a second, if maybe my parents had been speaking to her? They had her number. It wouldn't have been hard for them. They'd have said they were worried about me and told her what was going on. Maybe they'd even asked if we'd fallen out or something. I felt a hot flash of anger at the idea of it. I didn't know whether it was true or not, but my parents were protective and big-time worry guts. They'd never butted into my life before, but I'd never been in a terroristic hate crime against my sexuality before either. Unprecedented events call for unprecedented actions.

"How are you?" she asked, filling in the silence between us.

I shrugged. I didn't know what to say. My voice had turned into a little mole and was trying to bury its way back in the ground.

"O-K," Brittany said, slowly. Sarcastically. As kind as she was, she had no patience whatsoever. I thought of me feeling as though I missed her earlier on, pining for our friendship once more. What a joke.

She would never understand. I knew I could take her hand right now and pull her into an empty classroom and spill my guts out. Tell her everything. Nathan, my lies, how I hadn't been coping. The nightmares, the flashbacks, the voice. Me hurting myself.

I could do it. She wouldn't hold these weeks of silence against me. She would just hold me. She would stroke my hair and tell me that we're going to skip school today and get ice cream. Then, she'd stand next to me while I told my parents about it all.

But I didn't do that. Because I knew she'd never understand. She was there at Pride, but she wasn't the one being hurled abuse at. She wasn't the one who that man had wanted to kill. She didn't know. She'd never know.

We were silent for a second. She tried to play the waiting game with me, but I still wouldn't talk. We stayed like that, awkwardly standing in the school hallway, until the bell rang.

Brittany sighed and flopped her arms to her side. "Look, Lucy," she started. I felt a jolt go through me at being called Lucy rather than Luce. "I've been trying to give you space, but I miss you like crazy. I don't know what to do or say other than I'm here for you."

"I know," I muttered.

Brittany sighed again. It aggravated me to no end. It felt like I was being told off rather than supported.

"Can we please maybe go to lunch together, or something?" she blurts out. I felt her frantic energy between us. Her eyes were round and glossy, staring at me. If she wasn't so nervous about being late for class, she might have been crying.

"Yeah," I said. "Yeah. Of course we can."

"OK," she said. She tried to smile. "I'm sorry."

"Don't be," I said. "I'll see you at lunch."

"OK. I love you. I've really missed you."

I stared at her, blank. "I've gotta get to class."

The hurt on her face registered immediately before she covered it up with a small smile. Anyone else, someone who didn't know her so well, wouldn't have seen it. But I had Brittany down. I could read her like a book, even if I was blind.

"See you at lunch, then," she said. She began to walk off, the opposite direction to me.

I felt the words '*I love you too*' sit on the tip of my tongue, wanting to shout over to her before she was out of earshot. But I couldn't make them leave me.

I walked away. The hallways were pretty much empty now. I dragged my feet, not caring how late I was at all. It was an awful start to the term, but who gave a shit, really? I was an awful friend. I was an awful person. I wasn't sure that I liked this version of myself. Of who I was becoming.

My first lesson of the day was English Literature. I'd supposed to have read *Hard Times* by Charles Dickens over the summer holidays, but I hadn't. I'd planned on doing most of my homework in the last few weeks, as I always did. After Pride, is what I told myself. If only I'd known…

Outside the classroom, I heard my teachers echoing voice. My classmates were answering questions and talking about what they thought of *Hard Times*. I held my breath, hating making an entrance, and opened the door. I looked down at my feet as I walked in, letting the door squeak behind me. I only looked up again when I realised that everyone has gone completely silent. It had gone so quiet that a piece of dust could drop and we would've all been able to hear it.

Everyone stared at me. Their eyes wide and bulging. One girl, near the back, even started to cry. My face twisted, confused and angry and unsettled. I had always hated being the centre of attention, but this was on another level. This was freaky.

After what felt like forever, the classroom burst with noise. My ears began to rang with the loudness.

"Oh, Lucy, are you OK?"

"I can't believe what happened to you!"

"Did you get shot?"

"Is your arm OK?"

"Lucy, Lucy, please, are you OK?"

"Did you see him?"

"What did the gun look like?"

"No one heard from you! We thought you'd been

killed!"

"My Mum heard from your Mum that you've been struggling, are you OK, Lucy?"

"They've locked him up, you're safe!"

"I still can't believe someone had a gun!"

"STOP IT!" I bellowed.

My voice vibrated throughout the room. It silenced everyone. They all stared at me. Looking at them like this, shocked and bemused, they all looked one and the same. I wanted to keep screaming at them, but my ears began to ring even louder.

I turned around and pulled the door open, struggling as I did so. My hands started to shake violently. I realised that my heart was beating faster than it ever had and it was making my chest hurt. Fear flooded through me with the thought that maybe something was wrong with me.

I ran to the nearest girls bathrooms and locked myself in a stall. I slammed my backpack and slid down on the floor. That was something I'd never normally do, grossed out by the idea of bathroom germs on me.

I put my head between my knees. I was hyperventilating and my heart kept going faster. It felt as though the blood was disappearing from my body, pumping into nowhere by my ever-quickening heart. My head felt slightly woozy and my stomach felt sick.

But what really scared me was how much I felt as though I couldn't breathe. I closed my eyes and tried to focus on the ins and outs of my breathing, but all I could see were their faces. All I could hear were their voices.

I didn't know how long it lasted. How long I sat there and let the immensity of my emotions take over me. It could have been minutes. It could have been hours. I felt like death.

When it felt as if I'd finally managed to get a hold on my own breathing once more, I lifted myself off the floor.

My legs were shaking. All of me was shaking. I didn't want to go back there. I didn't want to do any of this day. I didn't want to be at all.

You should just-

Don't. Don't talk to me. Not right now. Please.

I left the bathroom. I walked through the quiet, empty hallways and tried not to cast any suspicion on myself. To me, I stuck out, sore and throbbing. But I must've been inconspicuous, invisible, because I managed to walk out onto the school fields and sneak through the fence.

I started to walk the way to home. My parents would both be at work. No one would even notice that I'd skipped. I didn't even care if they did. I didn't care if Brittany was upset that I'd skipped lunch with her. I didn't care if they rang my Mum and asked where I was.

All I wanted, in that moment, was to disappear. That was all I cared about.

Pride

7

After that, I started noticing all the little things people did differently around me now.

People looked at me with doleful eyes the hallway. Teachers asked me if I was 'feeling any better'. My parents never made me do any chores. Classmates who I'd never spoken to sat next to me in lessons.

All around me, I was being treated like I'd been remoulded into a glass figurine. The only person who treated me like I was a regular human being was Nathan.

I knew it was because I hadn't told him about Pride. He didn't know I was a lesbian. He didn't know anything about me, other than the carefully curated self I chose to show him. It was either that, or have no respite from the looks and the comments.

And fucking hell did I want a break from the looks and comments.

Weeks went by. I got my cast taken off my arm. I knew it would be gross, the accumulation of weeks' worth of unwashed sweat and dirt. But seeing it get taken off was surreal. My arm had healed. It didn't even hurt. There was barely a mark to show what it had been through.

But my brain hadn't. I could hang out with Nathan all I wanted. It didn't stop the screaming voices of bleeding people getting shot in my sleeping brain. The panic still attacked me with seemingly random words and triggers. There were now several patches of crescent moons on my body. My favourite to dig into was still the one Brittany carved out herself. It was the most real. But it wasn't always the most accessible part of myself to cling onto. I had to resort to other places, my legs being favourable and inconspicuous.

I hated doing it. It made me feel like I was... one of the depressed kids, or something. The ones you read about in the paper, or hear about in statistics on the news. *This just in, a staggering 13% uprise of depression diagnoses in teenagers...*

Never in my life had I ever pictured myself being in that statistic. I was always so good. So fine. I was Lucy. Plain old Lucy, with a nice house and nice parents and a fantastic best friend to boot. Good, stable grades. Healthy diet (aside from when binge-watching *Pretty Little Liars* on Netflix with Brittany).

I wasn't the kind of person who self-harmed. Or was depressed. Or who had repeating nightmares about a crazy man bellowing slurs before shooting me in the head.

But, as it turned out, the doctor had a radar for that kind of thing. At my appointment to take off the cast, he asked me how I'd been doing lately.

It was in the same voice that all the teachers and classmates and every-fucking-one around seemed to use. Poor little crazy Lucy. Is she *OK*?

I was sitting across from her on something akin to a cheap hospital bed. I'd been lying there, getting the cast sawn off my arm. In the corner of my eye, I could see the remnants of its discard on the metal tray. It had served such a purpose. It had held my arm together, perfectly, while my bones healed. And now it was just there. A nothing. Off to the bin once I'd left the room.

My Dad was with me, as Mum had been unable to get the day off work to come to the appointment. I hadn't minded. It wasn't exactly going to be riveting. I hadn't understood why my Dad had wanted to come in with me.

But, with Dr. Harper sat across from me asking me how I was, I understood why.

Paranoia set in once more. The same way it had with Brittany. My parents had so obviously talked to her about my state. My nightmares. Our friendship. Who's to say it isn't possible they somehow managed to speak to Dr. Harper, too?

You think too much of yourself.

... How so?

Thinking that everyone cares enough about you to ring doctors and talk to your friends.

My parents care. They care about me. I know they do.

Whatever you tell yourself.

...

"Lucy?" Dr. Harper said. "Are you off somewhere else? I'm not that boring, am I?"

She smiled at me. Her teeth were a dazzling white. She was young in her face, barely wrinkled, but she had that safe mothering energy about her. On her left hand, a simple gold band ring. It looked worn and loved. Like she'd been married for years.

I wondered if I would ever get married. If it'd be to a girl.

"No," I replied, snapping myself out of my head. I laid it on myself. I had to give the impression I was OK. Like I did with everyone else.

"I asked you how you'd been doing lately?"

"Oh," I said. "I've been fine. I'm fine. My arm is fine."

"Yes, your arm has healed wonderfully," Dr. Harper agreed. "But I was wondering about *you*. Your mood. Your schoolwork. Your eating and sleeping."

"Uh... I'm fine. My grades are fine. I have university application deadlines soon," I told her, a conscious attempt to be open. People who are open about how they feel aren't hiding anything about how they feel, right?

Dr. Harper nodded, but her eyes squinted at me. "Lucy," she started. "Would you perhaps like your Dad to leave the room?"

I hesitated for a split second. I could ask him to leave. It would be polite. He wouldn't mind. I could tell this doctor everything that was going on with me. It could be better.

But instead, I said, "No. It's fine. He's fine."

"OK," she said. "So what about your eating and sleeping? How are they?"

I knew what she was trying to get at. I crossed my arms across my chest. It was still an instinctive defence method, despite not having had use of my arm for weeks.

I must've not answered for a beat too long, because my Dad decided to chirp in. "She hasn't been sleeping well. My wife and I often get woken up by her screaming."

"Screaming?" Dr. Harper asked, her eyebrows crossing. A mix of concern and questioning.

"Yes, Doctor," My Dad answered. "From her nightmares."

The nightmares. The fucking nightmares. It was one thing I couldn't hide from my parents. There was no way to control what happened underneath my eyelids when I was asleep.

Dr. Harper nodded before turning her attention to me. "Is that true, Lucy?"

I scoffed. "No. My Dad lied about me having nightmares where I wake the whole neighbourhood up screaming just so he could get prescribed sleeping pills to sell in his underground drug cartel."

"Lucy!" My Dad reprimanded, his voice low and

growling, shocked.

Dr. Harper interjected. "No, Mr. Brown, it's fine, really-"

"It is not!" My Dad replied, his voice calmer in tone when talking to the doctor. "You shouldn't speak to people like that, let alone someone who is trying to help you."

I felt my eyes roll. It was almost as if I didn't have command of them. They heard something stupid and started spinning like a bowling ball on its way to knock out some pins. The tension in the room felt worse for me doing it.

Part of me didn't care how they reacted. How my own father reacted. What this doctor thought of me. I used to give so much of a shit about what everyone thought. I'd pick apart the little bits of myself that I didn't like and amplify them in my head until they were too big to ignore. My boring hair, flat and colourless. My slightly yellow stained teeth from the hundreds of cups of tea I drank daily. The funny little mole on the left side of my nose that foundation could never seem to cover.

Now, I realised, no one gave a shit about these things like I did. Brittany didn't even realise I had a mole near my nose until I pointed it out to her one day, complaining about it.

No. The things people cared about was what almost got me killed. What got so many other people killed. I don't know why so many people care. So many people campaign against me. Tell me who I can't love. But they do. They care that I'm a lesbian.

You're not. Stop.

I am. I am. How could I not be?

Because of Nathan.

He complicates things in a different way. I know I'm a lesbian. I've always known.

Are you proud, or something?

I... don't... I'm not proud, I just... I know what I am, I guess...

Sounds like you're proud. And pretty damn adamant. That sort of thing gets you killed.

Shut up.

The voice in my head was really starting to piss me off sometimes. I hated it. I hated how I couldn't turn it off. I always had to respond. Have a conversation. I wanted to try to vow to myself that I wouldn't reply to it when it spoke, but it was enticing. It was my very own, personal bully. You couldn't help but get bullied by bullies. They made you feel small. They made you feel like you deserved it.

"Lucy?" Dr. Harper said. Her voice was distant. My eyes were unfocused. I realised that the room had become blurry around the edges. "Do you always have this much trouble concentrating?"

'This much trouble concentrating'... Who does this bitch think she is?

Shut up.

"No. Yes. I don't know," I said. My words felt jumbled and mashed up. I wanted to spit them out like bad tasting food. "Sometimes. Lately, I guess."

"Is it affecting your schoolwork?"

Schoolwork. It always comes down to the schoolwork, somehow. Is that all people give a shit about? Is it all people think teenagers do? Fuck friendships. Fuck relationships. Let's only ever focus on schoolwork!

"I don't know," I said. She looked slightly disappointed for a second. Or perhaps it was annoyance. I couldn't tell. I'd been in here far longer than my appointment time by now.

"That's OK," Dr. Harper assured, despite the look on her face saying none of this was OK at all. "And you're having trouble sleeping, too, yes?"

"Yes. I have nightmares most of the time."

"OK," she said. "And how has your mood been?"

"Fine."

For a second, she looked over to my Dad. Pleading with him. *Tell me something more,* her eyes said, *because there's no way this stubborn bitch will.*

"Have you thought about getting any sort of counselling?" Dr. Harper suggested, realising I wasn't going to expand on my 'fine'.

"For what?" I asked.

She tried sympathy, a smile, warm. "You've been through something very difficult, Lucy. It's plain to both me and your loved ones that you're struggling with what happened. You don't need to suffer alone."

My body started to shake. I didn't want to think about anything Dr. Harper was suggesting. Counselling was for people who really needed it. Not me. I wasn't *that* bad. I had a couple nightmares. I scratched my arm until it bled every so often. I got so anxious that it turned into a panic attack sometimes.

Don't forget your self-destructive fake relationship with a boy...

Shut up.

But it wasn't... I wasn't... suicidal. I wasn't suicidal or anything. Sure, I'd had that stint where I'd lain in bed for a week, but I wasn't... *depressed*.

It was the first time I had truly thought about it. That all this stuff, things that had become normal for me, weren't actually normal at all. As much as you could define normal, anyway.

I wasn't healthy. Something *was* wrong.

But that didn't mean I was ready to accept it.

"I don't want counselling." I said, my voice firm.

Dr. Harper started, "Now, Lucy-"

My Dad then started, "Why don't you just think about it?"

"No." I said, cutting them both off. "I don't need it. I don't want it."

Silence iron-blanketed the room. I felt my heart palpitate beneath my ribs. It hurt. I tried to take in deep breaths, slow as to not draw more attention to myself than what was already on me.

"OK," Dr. Harper resigned. "I understand that counselling isn't something you want right now. If you change your mind-"

"I won't."

"If you change your mind," she continued, unphased by my interjection. "I recommend you make an appointment with your GP to talk about your options."

"Well, thanks, but-"

It was Dr. Harpers' turn to interrupt me. "Lucy," she said, her voice deeper. "What happened to you wasn't your fault. You deserve help if you need it. Your doctor might be able to help you with your sleeping issues. Promise me that you will at least think about it."

"OK," I promised.

I didn't know if I was lying to her. Maybe I would think about it. It wasn't the worlds' worst idea. It would be nice to be able to sleep a little more soundly. As I walked out the room, my Dad trudged by my side, I felt so unsure. I couldn't even talk to my own best friend about what was going on with me, let alone some stranger.

But I didn't know. I didn't know anything. It all felt blurry and disconnected. I wasn't there. Nothing was.

Pride

*

After the doctor's appointment, I tried even harder to keep my head down. I thought I'd been trying hard anyway, but I clearly hadn't been.

I started sleeping less. My theory was that if I didn't sleep, I wouldn't get nightmares. If I didn't get nightmares, I wouldn't wake up my parents. If I didn't wake up my parents, they wouldn't worry about me.

It was harder to concentrate on my piles of schoolwork without sleep. I was always someone who had to get her eight hours in or else I could not function. I started to take power naps when I got home from school to try to make it easier, but it made it harder.

I went to all my lessons. I put my head down. I did the work. My body was exhausted, my brain even more so. It was just about manageable. But the extra essays and homework and revision that all had to be done after school were not manageable.

Lying to my parents about being on top of stuff sucked. I tried to frame it to myself that I was protecting them from my pain and their pain. They wouldn't feel disappointed with my slowly dropping grades. But I knew it was bullshit. I just wanted to get through the day, any way possible. Even if that meant a few lies to both them and myself.

Between lessons, I'd exchange a few pleasantries with Brittany whenever I saw her. Normally, before, we'd hang out in the breaks and at lunch. We'd go to the cafeteria and eat whatever shitty hot food the school cooks had made for us. Sometimes it wasn't even that shitty. We'd pretend to be two celebrity food critics, putting on fake American accents and judging the all food.

"This tomato sa-WAR-ce is to-W-tally wa-RRRR-tery!"

"I know! And this pa-R-sta? Ta-R-lk about overdone!"

The memory still makes me smile.

Now I didn't know what she did at lunch. It wasn't like I went to the cafeteria anymore. I didn't want to eat the shitty food without her. I barely wanted to eat much, anyway. My clothes were beginning to wear me instead of me wearing them.

I wondered who she hung out with now. If she'd clung onto the myriad of acquaintances she'd made in her classes. I only ever saw her in passing, in corridors between the bell that rang for lessons.

Our conversations - if you could call them that - would always be a variant of the same.

"Hey!" Brittany would say, somewhat breathless and exasperated. She'd be holding more books then she could carry. I always used to tell her to just go to her locker or buy a backpack. She said that lockers and backpacks were for nerds.

"Hi," I'd say back.

"I, uh, I've really gotta go, but-"

"I-"

"You're OK, yeah?"

The bustle would stop for a moment, passing by in slow-motion. Every time she asked me if I was OK was an opportunity. If I said yes, we'd resume the same awkwardness. The same in-between state of *are we still friends? What's going on?*

If I said no, the in-between state would be over.

She never tried to confront me about why I didn't come to lunch that day. Maybe she'd gotten told that I ran out on class and presumably ran out on her, too. But she didn't text me either. There was no concern or worry. It kind of hurt me, which was stupid. It wasn't as if I'd tried to text her to tell her I couldn't make it. I didn't give her the decency, so she didn't give me it, either.

Brittany was good at pettiness. Be mean to her? She'll be mean right back. There was no high road in Brittany's world.

But I thought with me it was different. She wasn't afraid to back down from a fight with me. Sure, she'd give it what she could. It wouldn't be her if she didn't. But I really thought that with me, she would've tried harder.

It made me angry. Irrationally so, but still angry. Angry that she'd give up on me, our friendship, the years, so fucking easily.

So I'd say yes. Every time we bumped into each other and had our rehearsed dance of a conversation, I'd say yes.

"Yeah, I'm OK."
"Good."
"Yeah."
"OK, well, I really gotta-"
"Yeah-"
"OK-"
"See you then."
"Uh-huh, bye."

I started to feel lonelier because of it. I was so used to always having a friend around. Brittany and I would hang out whenever we could at school. Then we'd go to one of each other's houses and hang out some more. If we weren't together, we'd be texting. It was difficult going from that to nothing but hanging out with my parents eating dinner and watching Countdown.

So I texted Nathan. A lot. Pretty much constantly.

how was school today? :) x

OK. Stressful. Lots of homework. You? x

same lol. a-levels suck.

...

hows that uni application going x

Good! I think I've finally got my five choices. x

Lies upon lies upon lies.

We would video call, too, whenever I had the energy. He helped me to forget about my schoolwork and to laugh. He would tell me about his day and I'd lie about mine. Sometimes, he would fall asleep on the call with me. It felt horribly intimate.

Nathan was often busy with schoolwork and I was busy pretending to do schoolwork. In the few times we'd managed to see each other, we always had a good time. Watching movies in the cinema that were crap and talking too loudly the whole way through. Going on cafe tours in the entirety of Greater London and the surrounding areas, compiling a list of what places we loved most. (Side note: nothing had beaten the orange cafe full of books in Crawley on our first date. Meeting. Not date. Meeting. *Meeting!*)

But then, at the end of the meetings, he would always try to kiss me. And I'd let him. Throughout the entire date, he would always try to hold my hand. And I'd let him.

I didn't know when I'd let it stop.
I didn't know anything.
I didn't know anything.

I didn't know anything.

8

"Do you think my Mum will like this one, or this one?"

Nathan stood before me, holding two pairs of almost identical looking socks. I really didn't care what socks she would like more. I had no idea why he bothered to ask me either. It wasn't as if I'd ever even met the woman.

"I don't know," I admitted. "That one."

I pointed toward the one that slightly less fluffy and pink. Gross. Nathan smiled, gleeful. He held the pair of overly expensive socks in one hand and took my own hand in his other. His fingers interlocked with mine as we walked toward the counter.

Christmas was fast approaching. Both of us had left our Christmas shopping until the last minute; which was typical of me as I hated shopping. Especially *Christmas* shopping. Everywhere was ten times more crowded than it usually was. It was all sweaty bodies cramped together, long lines at checkouts, sardine-packed buses getting from one high street to another.

This was all exemplified by the fact Nathan, clutching to the fact I lived barely within London, chose to shop at Oxford Street. Which was hell any normal day of the year. But in the Christmas season? It made hell look like a summer holiday to the Bahamas.

We stood in the queue together, my hand getting clammy. I tried to tell myself that it was kinda nice that I was hanging out with Nathan. Outside the house. Doing something. On a weekend. It felt like weeks had gone by, wilting away in my bed or in classrooms, without some proper socialising. Going to cafes and video calling with

Nathan every so often felt too much like second nature to compare them this.

"Are you sure she'll like them?" Nathan asked as we got closer to the cashier.

My feet hurt from too much walking and standing. "Yes. They'll be fine." I said, blunt.

"She really loves stuff like this, you know," he continued. "But she has so many pairs that they're all basically just odds now-"

"Uh-hm."

"So it'll be nice for her to have a proper pair-"

"Yeah."

"And they're such good quality-"

"Hmm."

"Maybe she won't *want* to lose this pair!"

I stared off into the distance. Maybe if I stopped talking, then he'd stop talking. I let my eyes go a little blurry, trying to wash the sound of annoying Christmas shoppers off me. My feet did the walking for me as I dozed off into a disconnected state.

I felt very much wrong to ever think this was going to be good for me. I knew I hated shopping, yet I tried to convince myself that somehow Nathan would make it bearable. It was busy and loud and I was so fucking tired.

And I had to admit it to myself - it was difficult. It was difficult being around such a vast amount of people, crowded together in such a way. The smell of the sweat rolling off their skin, the blurred together chatter, reminded me of being back in that hall. Stuck, with the doors closed, desperate. Sometimes, I was sure I could hear the start of the screaming in the back of my head somewhere.

All I wanted was to go home. To get back into bed and go to sleep. To ignore my overgrown pile of homework sheets and practise exams. To forget about the sheet I needed my Mum to sign to say I got a fail in my last English mock.

I wanted to be nothing.

When we left the shop, with the socks wrapped in a paper bag, Nathan turned to me. "Are you feeling OK?"

Oh, for fuck...

I know.

You're not hiding it well enough. Again.

I know.

"Yeah." I said. "I mean, no. I don't know. It's just so busy here. I can't hear myself think."

Nathan smirked, almost a little relieved. "I get that," he said. "Why don't we have a break?"

"OK."

"A cafe?" He smiled, thinking it was the best idea in the world. After all, cafes were *our thing* now.

"OK."

We walked off the high street and into quieter alleyways. I preferred the run-down, about to run out of business sort of cafes. Places like that, as I pointed out, always made the best tea because it was the same as the sort of stuff you'd get at home.

"But what's the point?" Nathan had asked when I explained this. "If you could get tea at home, why wouldn't you get it at home?"

"You can get movies at home, yet we all go to the cinema."

"They're new releases, though."

"Tea doesn't *have* new releases."

"You make *zero* sense," Nathan had said, a jokey smile on his face. I remembered distinctly the look in his eyes. Doey, soft. Falling.

Falling for me.

After some directionless walking, we found a hidden

little corner cafe in a dodgy street. It was painted an ice-y shade of green, bordered with white. A bell rang, echoing as we walked through the door. Inside wasn't nearly as newly decorated. The tables were similar to the foldable wooden ones you'd find in exam room halls and the chairs were mismatched stools.

My fingers had a welcome sting from the change of cold to heat. Choosing a two-seater table close to the wall, I took off my khaki coat and tucked it underneath the stool.

"What would you like?" I asked Nathan.

He sat down across from me and twisted his neck to face the chalk-written menu board. "Uhh…" he deliberated. "I think I'll have one of the Christmas specials."

"Christmas specials? This place is fancy," I said. Nathan laughed. I felt a little lighter now I was out of the crowds, but still tired. I knew I would have to order a coffee. The caffeine hit would be the only thing that would get me through the rest of that day.

He's only laughing at you because he's just glad you're not being all gloomy anymore.

Shut up.

No one wants to hang out with the boring, depressed girl.

Shut up.

You'll lose your fake boyfriend if you're not careful.

SHUT UP!

"Hmm… I think I'll have the mint hot chocolate." he said. "Or the gingerbread spiced latte. No. Mint hot chocolate."

I rolled my eyes. I was glad he couldn't see me. "You'll have the mint hot chocolate." I said. One thing I'd learnt about Nathan, that I couldn't stand, was that he was incredibly indecisive. It made me feel controlling, picking things for him, but I felt as though he'd be deliberating all day if I didn't.

The man behind the counter looked happy to see me as I approached him. Friendly. Proud. Another thing I loved about these cafes was the amount of love that normally went into them. Chains could never compete with it.

"Hi," I said. I put a little extra effort into making mouth upturn into a smile. "Can I get a coffee and a mint hot chocolate, please?"

"Sure thing," he replied. His accent was thick and hard to place. "Would you like whipped cream with the hot chocolate?"

"Uh, yeah, sure," I answered. Another decision of Nathan's that was easier to answer for him.

I waited at the counter for the server to make our drinks. He placed them on a glass tray, sprinkled chocolate flakes onto the hot chocolate. My coffee came with a small milk jug and a bowl of white sugar cubes. With warmth, I thanked him, gave him the money and popped the change into the tip jar. I didn't have a part-time job or any other way of income besides cards on birthdays, but I didn't care. This guy, and the others like him, deserved it.

You don't deserve anything.

I know.

Balancing the tray carefully (my healed arm hadn't fully regained its strength), I brought the drinks over to our table. There was only a two other pairs of customers in the cafe with us and it makes the atmosphere a little awkward. I felt as if everyone could hear me talking.

"Ahhh, thanks." Nathan said, barely letting me put down the tray before eagerly taking the cup. He sipped from his drink, steam rising over his face, letting out a sound of pleasure as the chocolatey taste hit his tongue.

"Good, I presume?"

"Mmmm," he murmured. "You have no idea. Over there with your bitter coffee."

"Coffee isn't so bad."

Nathan grimaced. "It's only ever OK at best. And that's when you add five sugars and full-fat milk."

I let out a small laugh. "I guess you're kinda right there." I responded as I started to add two cubes of the sugar into the small cup and a dash of the milk. "But it still tastes good. And I need the caffeine."

"Oh," Nathan said, raising an eyebrow. "Why's that?"

You idiot, the voice in my head said. *You're supposed to seem fine.*

I know, sorry. Sorry.

"Oh, I didn't sleep that well last night. Dad was snoring *so* loudly," I lied. "I thought he'd swallowed a hippo."

Nathan snorted. He'd only started laughing in that I-don't-need-to-fake-myself anymore way in the last few weeks. I could imagine how someone else would feel lucky to hear such a laugh. Realising they were being fallen in love with, and falling in love right back.

But not me. I felt so fucked up.

I could remember my first ever proper crush on a girl. Not just liking Sally Holden in Year 3, wishing she'd play kiss chase with me.

My first proper crush was on a girl in one of my GCSE science classes. Her name was Georgie. She had shiny hair that I was sure had to have been dyed that colour. No natural brown looked so chocolatey. Her eyes shone blue, almost lost in the sea of freckles that crowded her nose like people at a concert. My stomach flipped around her, twisting in that painful but wonderful way.

Pride

For one term, we were class partners, meaning whenever we did experiments, we did them together. I still remember how it felt as though my heart had truly and physically stopped when she accidentally touched my hand.

I had none of that with the boy who sat across from me. He drank his hot chocolate, his cheeks and nose red from the cold. Over the rim of his mug, he smiled at me with his eyes. He was beautiful. Undoubtedly so. But I didn't feel anything for him.

Nathan slammed down his mug, pulling me away from my rose-tinted memories of Georgie. "That was amazing," he proclaimed.

"Must've been. You finished it in record time."

"Heh. Yeah. What can I say? Mint and chocolate go so well together," he smiled.

I murmured in agreement, sipping on my coffee. It burnt my tongue. I always had to wait until it cooled to drink it, subsequently earning me the teasing of being a 'coward' from Nathan.

"You know what else goes well together?" Nathan asked.

"Hmm?"

"Me and you."

Oh God. That was the corniest thing I'd ever heard. I wondered how long he'd been planning that one.

I couldn't let my disdain show, so I tried to smile. He reached his hand across the table, pushing his empty mug away, and reached for my hand. He twisted his fingers around mine, playing with them. I hated when he did that.

His doleful eyes poured themselves into mine. "Lucy…" he started.

I felt a surge of anxiety hit the pit of my stomach. It began to twist, like our fingers. "Yes?" I asked.

"We've been hanging out for a while," he continued.

"And I've been... I've had a lot of fun. I'm *having* a lot fun. I just think you're, like, this amazing person. I... Man, I'm really not doing very well at this, am I?"

"Well what at?" I questioned. Twist, twist, twist.

"I'm just gonna say it."

"OK."

"Will you be my girlfriend?"

I knew it was coming, but I still felt like a pin getting struck out by a bowling ball. Breath left my chest as I stared right back at him and his vulnerable gaze. His heart was laid open on the table, beating frantically. My guts were piled out on the floor, spiralling out of control.

Speak, speak!

...

You can't say nothing!

....

Say yes! Be normal! Be the Lucy you want to be!

I... What if I don't want this? I don't want to hurt him. I don't want that.

You know what you don't want. You know what you fear. It'll hurt him if you say no. This could be your becoming.

I don't know...

Say yes!

...

SAY YES!

"Yes."

His face immediately brightened. It transformed into joy that I didn't think was possible, unless you were an toddler getting Lego on Christmas day.

He sat at the table for a moment, his mouth blubbered, unsure of what to say next. So he didn't say anything. He got up and came straight over to me and started to hug me.

I was now the girlfriend of someone I didn't love. I

didn't even like. I could never even like.

I couldn't understand. How had he fallen for me, so much, so easily? We hung out a lot. We talked a lot. We were good friends, always had a laugh. And sure he'd met my parents and stuff, but it wasn't as if we'd even kissed yet. Every time it seemed as though he was leaning in for that sort of thing, I'd go for the hug instead. I thought that was probably a good thing on my end, an attempt at some sort of friend zone.

But I guess not.

Maybe this was his attempt at working out if I liked him for real. In the same way he liked me. If I said yes, then hooray! He wasn't in the friendzone.

And now I had said yes. And he wasn't in the friendzone at all.

He was my boyfriend. I was a lesbian with a boyfriend.

A fucking lesbian with a boyfriend!

He kept hugging me. His all-enveloping arms wrapped so tightly around me. It started to constrict my chest as he pulled me in harder and harder.

It was a 'oh, thank god' hug on his end, but on mine, all I could think about was my own body, being jam-packed in the hall at Pride. How little I'd been able to breathe between the mounds of pushing people, trying to escape. Trying to live.

Within moments of thinking about Pride and the crowd, I felt panic. A tsunami of it, rising and pulling me under, water filling my lungs. I felt nauseous. A hurricane of it, swirling around my stomach, wreaking havoc on every important part of my body.

I had to get out of this. I didn't know what I meant by this, the hug, being his girlfriend… I just had to go. Right then.

I pushed away, sharply. "I have to go."

Nathan's previous elation drained from his face. "What?"

"I have to go." I repeated. The words felt hard to get out, and I was wheezing as I'd just ran a mile.

"Why? What's happened?"

I must've looked so fucking insane, eyes must've been wild and high. "I just have to go. I forgot…"

"Forgot what?"

"I… I have to help my parents, with packing, I…"

Nathan grabbed onto my shoulder. It was an innocent gesture, harmless. So harmless. It was caring. But I flinched. The hurt registered on his face, and I remembered how I'd done the same thing to him the day we met in the hospital.

"Sorry. God. I'm sorry."

"I don't understand what's happening…" Nathan said. His voice was so small.

I tried to breathe a little. It didn't work very well, but it cleared my head for a moment. A moment was all I needed. "I completely forgot about how I promised I'd help them pack up some stuff in the loft today. It's a three-man job at the least. They'd been making me promise this for weeks," I explained. Lies, lies, lies.

"I can help, if you want?" Nathan asked, his eyes a little more hopeful. "Honestly, I don't mind. And your parents were so nice, it'd be great to see them again."

I shook my head, vehemently. "No, no, really, it's fine," I said. "And besides, they'd know I'd skived on all that packing fun to be with you if you came along."

He still looked confused. And hurt. I tried to imagine him, tried to imagine being behind his eyes. This strange girl. I'd come into his life in a flash, taken over, broken into his thoughts and I was… *playing* with him. Like I was a cat, and he was the mouse I knew I was going to kill but wanted a little fun with first.

"I'm really sorry," I repeated.

"It's OK," Nathan said, taking his turn in lying. He'd probably been planning on asking me to be his girlfriend for weeks. And here I was, freaking out all over the place.

"No, please," I insisted. "Please. I'm sorry I acted so odd then, I... I just remembered suddenly and I got freaked out. I'm not the sort of person who bails on her family when they need her."

No, but you are the sort of person who lies and crushes people's feelings...

...

Nathan smiled. It was half-hearted, but a little real. "OK. I get that."

He wanted to believe me. He wanted to think I was better than the person I clearly was. It was possible he might've been romanticising me a little bit. Forgiveness came too easily in his eyes.

Be nice. Be good. Rectify this. You were doing so well.

...

"I... Thanks. For asking me. I've been waiting for that." I said.

It wasn't strictly a lie. I had been waiting for it. I knew it was going to happen one day, especially if we kept holding hands and kissing cheeks. But I hadn't been waiting for it in the way I'd implied.

"You better get going," Nathan grinned. "Lots of packing to do." I think I fixed it. My head told me that that was good. My heart wanted to fucking destroy itself. I got the urge to dig my fingernails into my arm, my leg, into anywhere there was skin.

"Yeah," I agreed. "Anyway, thanks for helping me get all my Christmas shopping done."

"You too," he said. "Honestly, I wouldn't have gotten it done without you. I'm awful at it."

I faked a smirk. "Same. Well… see you."

He pulled me in for another hug. I held my breath the entire three seconds it lasted.

And when he started to pull away, he only let a few inches between us. He turned his head to mine and kissed me. His lips parted between my own, warm and soft. The tip of his nose, still a little frosted from the December cold, touched my cheek.

It was over as quickly as it started. His cheeks flushed red. Happiness or embarrassment or a mix of both. I tried to copy his expression.

As I left the cafe, we said bye once more, awkwardness hanging between us. A new couple. Having their first kiss.

The door closed behind me. The bell rang out once more. It rang through me, bouncing off my empty body and brain.

Empty, empty, empty.

*

It starts in a dark room.

I know exactly what room it is. I know exactly where I am.

The stage is ahead of me, lights beaming down. If he was here, the lights would be spotlighted on him.

Normally, when I'm in this room, I'm surrounded by them. The suffocating mass of bodies. I'd be drowning in sound. Piercing, eardrum shattering screaming. Pain, pain, pain!

But this time I'm not. I'm sat alone in darkness. Beneath me, a chair. Hard, stumpy. The same chair that I was sitting on in the cafe when Nathan asked me to be his girlfriend.

Nathan.

My heart clenches. It tears the fuck apart. It doesn't want to be in my chest anymore. I'm a liar. I'm disgusting. I'm hurtful, spiteful, mean. I'm ruining. It doesn't want to beat for someone like me. There are many people who need hearts and this is the body it was trapped in?

A losing hand in a game of blackjack.

People begin to materialise around me. Faces and shapes forming from the pitch darkness. Their mouths moving, but I can't hear them.

"What?" I hear myself asking. "What?"

I begin to pick out the faces. The first I see is Brittany.

Lip piercing to the left side, black hair swooping over her face. Her cheeks covered in holographic glitter. On her shirt, a rainbow pin. Pride Brittany.

"You left me! You let go of me! You left me!"

A searing hot pain. I didn't know where it hurt, but it rings through my body. Sizzling, sizzling, sizzling.

Brittanys eyes bore into me. She starts to melt. Her skin, melting off from the high points of her cheeks, into the ground. It left bones, but they're shapeless. Not a skull. Not a anything.

Before I can understand it, Nathan takes her place. His golden hair looks dark within the black room, his usual happy face replaced with disgust. Distaste. I was something so sweet tasting, until he sucked down to my core. Nothing but pure sour to find there.

"You're lying to me! You're hurting me! You're lying to me!"

He burst into fire. Anger, resentment. Before his entire being turns into nothing but ash, I see his once blue eyes turn red.

The hot poker pain hits me again. It encapsulates me in suffering.

In the wake of Nathans' smoke, a man appears. He's blurry, I don't know exactly what he looks like, but his presence is clear enough. He is the most evil. He condemns me. He is what greets you at the gates.

Clasped between his hands is a gun. He stands metres from me, but the gun is everywhere all at once, bigger than both he and I.

"You fucking faggot! You disgusting futile unhuman! You

fucking faggot!"

He pulls the trigger. The bullet rips through my flesh, tearing me into tiny pieces. I am wrong, wrong, wrong.

It is then silent. A second of silence. Repentance. Guilt.

I thought it had stopped.

Then they all came.

The bodies, hundreds of script less, nameless bodies. They aren't near me, but somehow they're compressing me. Every inch of my separated flesh being squished.

"You're alive, and I'm not! You should've died instead! You're alive, and I'm not!"

"You're alive, and I'm not! You're lying to yourself! You're alive, and I'm not!"

"You're alive, and I'm not! You don't deserve to live! You're alive, and I'm not!"

I'm alive, and they're not.
I'm alive, and they're not.
I'm alive, and they're not.

9

Christmas was one of my favourite holidays.

Our home was a cornucopia of festivity and merriment. Mum would decorate every available surface with a mix of tinsel and fairy lights. She would drape them around banisters, hang it off the ceiling and the door frames. Every morning leading up to the 25th, Mum would squirt a gingerbread and spice room spray. It made me want cookies.

But the Christmas tree was the real attraction. It always *had* to be real. One weekend before November, my parents would drag me down to a farm an hour's drive outside of London to pick a tree. We went to the same place every year for as long as I could remember. I knew we would do the same in the new house. Our new place wasn't going to be far away from our old home. But it still sucked. It still felt different.

Mum would decorate the tree the second it cracked midnight on December 1st. It took her hours to get it right, and she'd be so tired the next day. But she thought it was worth it. It was beautiful.

It wasn't one of those elegant looking trees. The perfect amount of baubles and tinsel, nothing tacky or overbearing. Nope. Mum put everything on the Christmas tree. Everything.

The crummy decorations I made in arts and crafts in school. Falling apart, mismatched bits of tinsel. An angel without her wings.

"People who buy their Christmas tree decorations are suckers!" Mum would joke.

Brittany loved it. She fully agreed with my Mum. She thought that the memories behind our Christmas were what made it special.

"My parents are so fucking elegant," she told me once. "It's all gold, silver and black in our house at Christmas. I fucking hate it. Lighten the fuck up! It's Christmas! Get drunk!"

'Get drunk' was Brittanys' motto during December. She went a little crazy every Christmas season. She used it as an excuse to party more and party harder. Exams often fell after the New Year, but she didn't care that she let the school priority slip a little bit. Besides, she was so good at finding ways to balance stuff. She could go to a party every weekend and still look fresh as a daisy on Monday morning with her A* worthy homework.

This Christmas, though, nothing was the same.

There was no real tree. No decorations because they'd gotten packed away and stored in some facility a couple miles away. And worst of all, there was no Brittany.

I always hated how mad she got with the alcohol and partying at Christmas, but I had really started to miss my best friend. This was the first year since knowing her that I hadn't bought her a present.

The worst part of it all was how much I felt like I needed a friend right now. Moving house was killing me. I hated seeing the house so derelict and empty of everything that made it my home.

On top of that, I was being texted by Nathan every second of every day. He was kinda clingy as a friend, but even more so as a boyfriend.

look at our christmas tree ! x
...

just got done with hw, u wanna video call? xxx
...
missing u. i still cant believe ur my girlfriend. <3
...
when we gonna meet up to exchange xmas presents? :P x

I felt mean, thinking that he was clingy. It was likely he was being a normal boyfriend, having a normal conversation with his normal girlfriend.
You're not exactly a normal girlfriend, though, are you?
...
Either way, it was annoying. All of it. I felt stressed and frayed, my nerves chewed on like raw meat.

"Lucy!" I heard my Mum calling from downstairs.

"What?" I bellowed, feeling lazy. I didn't want to go down there if it was something could be easily solved by shouting back.

"Come down here, please!"

I groaned before pulling myself out of the safe confines of my bed. It was where I spend most of my free time. Warm, soft, safe. My only risk was falling asleep, which was getting harder everyday anyway.

As I walked down the stairs, hand gripping bannister for stability, I took in the lack of Christmas. Tinsel had been replaced with packing boxes and unsettled dust. I wondered if it killed my Mum as much as me.

"Could you please help your Dad and I with all of this stuff?" My Mum asked when I reached her. She was standing in the living room where most of our books were now packed into small cardboard boxes. "The storage truck is going to be here in a couple minutes."

I nodded. There was no point saying anything back.

My parents knew how I felt about the house move. Before Pride, I used to talk to them a lot about what was on my mind. They knew I didn't want to go and how upset I was by it.

"This new place is going to so much smaller," My Mum had said, as if that was supposed to make it sound any better. "It'll be cheaper to heat up in the winters."

"And besides, Luce," My Dad had interjected. "We love this house as much as you, but it's time for a change. We've been in this one for twenty years. Even before you were born. We never wanted this to be our forever home."

I didn't understand that. Sure, they may not have wanted it to be, but what about me? Like it or not, it had become my forever home. I couldn't imagine opening presents on Christmas morning somewhere else. I couldn't imagine family dinners in anywhere other than our dining room. This new place didn't even *have* a dining room.

When the storage truck arrived to take our next load of stuff, my parents and I started to haul boxes into the back of it. It didn't take a long time, but it surprisingly hurt my back and arms.

I hunched over, clutching the low, sore spot of my back and groaning.

My Mum walked in. "Oh, Lucy, are you OK?!" she asked, frantic.

"Ack, yeah," I replied, but my voice was still too groan-y and in pain for her to believe me.

"Sit down, love, please," she said, ushering me to the sofa.

I sat, a little pain rippling through my spine. I clenched my teeth and tried not to show it. I knew it would pass. It was just a little back pain. I was only 17, but I swore I had the back of a 70 year old sometimes.

"What's wrong?" Mum badgered.

"A bit of back pain from lifting the heavy boxes," I

explained. "And my arm aches a little too. The healed one. It's still getting back it's muscle."

My Mum frowned. "Will you be OK? I'm sorry we asked for your help, love, it's just-"

"No, Mum, I understand, don't worry," I tried to sympathise. "It really isn't a big deal."

"Yes, but, Lucy..." she started.

"Hmm..."

"Your Dad and I have been a little worried by how much weight you've been losing. You barely eat anything at dinner and it really shows..."

"I don't think a little weight loss has impacted on my ability to pick up boxes and use a muscle in my back..."

My Mum went on as if I hadn't spoken. "...And we're concerned for your wellbeing. It's not good to lose so much weight in such a short time. And you've been having these nightmares. And the stuff with Brittany-"

"Mum-"

"-She used to be your best friend and now-"

Ding!

Saved by the bell.

"You better get the door," I said.

My Mum furrowed her brows at me. She was clearly a little pissed at the doorbell's timing. How long had she been planning to try to have a little heart to heart with me, I wondered.

I stayed half-sitting, half-lying down on our sofa. It was one of the few things left in the sitting room, only because my parents were buying a new one for the new house. No more sticky, sweaty butt on our old leather couch in the summer. Somehow, as much as I hated it, I'd miss it, too.

Running my fingers along the cracks of the leather, I hoped I'd get to leave soon and go back to bed. Maybe, with the door knocker, Mum would forget about her 'little chat' with me.

Then, Nathan walked into my living room. I was not expecting that.

We hadn't arranged to meet up or see each other, but there he was. Bundled up in a thick red coat with a cold red nose to match. In his gloved hands was a small box wrapped in gold wrapping paper with holly leaves printed on it.

"Hi," he said, breathing the greeting.

I sat up, slowly as to not hurt the aching pain in my back. I didn't want to give an involuntarily groan and have yet another person look at me as if I was breaking. "Hi." I said back.

"I'm sorry to drop in on you unannounced," he started. "But I wanted to surprise you. With this."

He held the present out to me, his smile barely able to hide his excitement. *Oh God*, I thought.

I took it from his hands, awkwardly fiddling with the small box between my hands. Nathan sat down next to me, too close, our knees touching. He was still smiling. It made my stomach twist.

"Well, are you gonna open it?" he asked.

"Y-yeah," I murmured. My fingers trembled slightly as I pulled apart the carefully wrapped gift. Inside the paper was a long, thin navy velveteen box.

"Open it, open it!" Nathan exclaimed. His hands were balling up parts of his coat with nervousness.

I twisted the silver clasp and opened the box. Inside was a necklace. It was gold, heart-shaped and had an engraved letter on it. An *N*.

N.

He wanted me to wear this. A brandishing of our fake relationship.

I thought I was going to be sick.

"I-"

"Do you like it?"

His voice was vulnerable. Open. Nervous. It was the same tone he used when he asked me to be his girlfriend.

Before I had the chance to reply, both of my parents walked into the living room.

"Ooh, what did he get you?" My Mum crooned, coming over towards us.

I didn't know how to speak. I couldn't let them see, but they were going to. They were going to see and this was going to happen and I wanted to explode.

They would know.

Would they figure it out? That I was… That I had a fake boyfriend? That Nathan was being… dragged along… and…

"Oh," My Dad said, confusion laced beneath the simple expression. "It's lovely, Nathan."

"Yes, it is," My Mum agreed, but her previous vigour was gone. Her vibrant smile had been wiped off her face, replaced with the same confusion as my Dad.

Nathan smiled at them. No, he beamed. He was so happy. It was pure and unfiltered and I was horrible. "Thanks," he said. "Lucy… do you like it?"

He turned back toward me, a little of the vulnerability slipping back in. I still hadn't said anything, but how was I supposed to react? I couldn't fake my way into making Nathan feel OK, hug him and kiss him again (*eurgh*). If I did any of that, my parents would know somethings up even more so than they already did.

I was stuck between a rock and a hard place.

I was stuck between a fucking engraved necklace and my parents who believed they had a lesbian daughter.

"I love it." I said, eventually. It was too long of a pause. Nathan looked so unsure. My parents matched.

Why can't you just be fucking happy?

How the fuck could I even try to be happy right now?

A boy loves you. He's got you an expensive gift. He's objectively attractive. People don't stare at you when you're with him.

I can't convince myself into liking him, or this gift. I can't, I can't, I can't.

You're not even trying.

"If you don't like it, you can tell me," Nathan said.

My parents stood over us. Their presence was so looming. They weren't usually the kind of parents who had to know every intimate aspect of your social life. But right now, I figured, they probably couldn't take their eyes away from this train wreck.

"I do. Sorry. I just didn't know you were coming over and I don't feel very well so I'm going to just… go… back to my bed…" I floundering over the words, tripping on the hills of my lies.

I pushed myself up from the sofa and through my parents. The necklace was still clutched in my hands, rattling around in its box. I didn't want to hear anything as I stumbled up the stairs.

I wasn't going to my bed, though. I went straight towards the bathroom and locked the door behind me. I pulled down the toilet seat and my trousers in a mismatched fumble before sitting down.

My legs were littered with scars and scabs from my fingernails. I stared down at it, wishing for more. Wanting more. God, I felt so fucking fucked up. I hated myself. I wanted to scream into the oblivion.

But I couldn't. So I grabbed one of my razors. Pink and barely used, I snapped it, uncaring if the blades hurt the palms of my hand.

It was difficult to break the plastic. They didn't really design the shavers to be broken like this, I guessed.

Eventually, though, it gave way a little. Enough.

Enough for me to get one of the razor blades to slice across the skin of my thigh. I felt the sharp metal sink into the flesh, blood dots rising shortly after. I tasted metal in my mouth, I felt blood in my stomach.

I wasn't OK.

*

The vibrations are gunshots in my pocket.

went home, hope u feel better soon. thinking of u <3

did u like the present? x

r u feeling any better? :)

really really hope you liked the necklace. it was so hard keeping it a secret lol xx

I didn't reply to any of them. I couldn't figure out how to.

My options were limited. I could do what I'd been doing since the moment I met him: lie. Lie about liking the gift. Tell him I'm wearing it right now and it's making me feel so much better for it. That I'm thinking of him, too, and how I hope he likes my gift. (Which, by the way, I didn't even think to get him a present. I am truly the worst human).

Or, I could tell him the truth. Or, an easier half-truth, which is what it would be. I couldn't stand to tell him the full extent of it all. That I'm gay and have been using him to make myself feel less anxious when walking down the street. No, instead, I would tell him that this was getting a bit too serious a bit too quickly and I wanted to end things.

But, in that moment, I was too cowardly to do either of those things. So, I did nothing instead.

I turned off my phone, disturbed by the constant vibrating. A niggling part of me knew it would likely make him more anxious, not replying, seeing that his messages won't even send. But it was the only thing I could do to keep myself sane. To keep myself breathing.

I laid back in my bed, pulling the duvet over my head. My leg stung from where the material of my jeans rubbed against it. I'd made only a few thin gashes, but the guilt felt immeasurable. The guilt felt worse than the cuts.

I knew I didn't need to be guilty about it. I was hurting and in pain and I needed help. I wanted to go back in time, to the girl sitting in Dr. Harper's office and scream at her. *Say something!* I would say. *Get help! You don't want to do this!*

But it was too late. It felt all too late. I was digging a hole that had no escape, and no one could hand me a ladder.

My parents knocked on the door. I wasn't sure how a knock could sound apprehensive, but they somehow managed it.

"Come in," I said, groggy. With reluctance, I peeled the duvet off my head. I had to keep up the 'I'm OK' act as much as I could, after all. No one believes that someone's OK if they spend their entire life in bed.

My Mum walked through first, my Dad followed after her. They clicked the handle shut behind them. Without invitation, they sat on the foot of my bed, back to back, but both facing me.

"Lucy?" My Mum asked, gingerly.

"Mmm."

"What's going on with Nathan?"

Fuck, shit, balls, bollocks, oh *God*, I don't want this. I don't want this. I DON'T WANT THIS.

"What do you mean?" I said.

"Come on, Luce," My Dad said. "We aren't dumb. Neither are you. We just want to know what's going on."

"We're a little confused, is all, sweet."

I could feel myself shaking, despite the fact I was boiling hot underneath this duvet. "He's... he's my boyfriend."

My parents started to look like little fish, blobbing and blubbering at this new revelation, unsure where to start.

"Boyfriend?" Mum asked, perplexed. She didn't bother trying to hide her confusion or misunderstanding. "I thought..."

"I don't understand..." Dad interjected.

"I know, I know," I muttered. I felt hotter, my blood rising in temperature. I was annoyed by them.

Their nosiness caused this. Their intrusion.

They were just... I dunno... excited to see what Nathan got me. They thought he was a friend of mine, after all.

It's their own fault. This confusion and hurt, their upset by your lies, it's their fault.

I don't... I don't think...

It's their own...

Please, stop. Please. I can't deal with you too.

"What do you mean he's your boyfriend?" Mum asked. "We thought... we thought you liked girls, sweetheart."

"I..." I stammered. Where the hell did I go from here? All of this was so much more complicated. Now it wasn't just Nathan and I. I hadn't planned any of this, I'd let it all happen, and now it was spiralling.

Dad took my hesitation as my confusion. "Are you

still questioning? Because it's OK to, Lucy. It can be a difficult thing to work out."

My Mum nodded along with him. I wondered if they'd talked about me.

Paranoid, paranoid, paranoid...

Shut up.

I wondered if they'd lain in bed together, wondering if there was a chance I was bisexual rather than a lesbian.

Maybe they'd prefer if you were.

... Maybe.

"I'm bisexual."

My voice said the words before my brain had a chance to command it to. It was a lie, obviously. I knew I wasn't bisexual. I'd never had a crush on a boy in my life. I couldn't even imagine what makes them attractive. I understood it, visually, but I never actually *felt* anything.

I was gay, of that I was sure, but what they wanted to hear would calm them down. They didn't want to know they had a liar for a daughter, someone who ruined a random boy's life for no real reason. They wanted something easy. A neat bow, to tie it all up, to answer the questions they hadn't wanted to ask.

For a few seconds, "Oh," was all they seemed to be able to manage to say.

Then, "Is this something you've realised?" My Mum asked.

I nod, moving my head minutely up and down.

"Oh."

"Was he your boyfriend this whole time?"

"No, no," I said. "Only since, like, a week ago really."

"Is this why Brittany and you aren't talking?" Dad asked.

I lifted my eyebrows. Had they been talking about

that together on their own, as well?

Paranoid, paranoid, paranoid.

Shut up.

P-a-r-a-n-o-i-d.

It's normal for parents to talk about their kid. Right?

PARANOID!

Shut the fuck up.

"No," I assured them both. "No. That's not why."

I could see from the looks in their hungry eyes that they wanted to ask more. Dig deeper, find out what's been going on with Brittany and I. But they didn't. They seemed to sense that if they tried any harder, I'd likely bite back soon.

"OK," Mum said, after a little while. She tried out a warm smile on me. Motherly. "Well, Lucy, as you know, we love you. Gay, straight, bisexual, whatever. As long as you're healthy and happy."

I tried to smile back. Lies, lies, lies.

"Exactly what your Mum said," Dad agreed. "And hey, now we know, we'd love to have him round for dinner again. Give him the boyfriend Treatment."

I could hear the classical movie straight teen girl, groaning but smiling at her parents. Happy they'd accepted she had a boyfriend. Normalised by a father giving him a 'hard time' because that's what Dads did to protect their daughters.

What a load of bullshit.

"Yeah." I said, eventually faking a smile too.

The lies feel like they're snowing me in. Fake smiles upon forced laughs. Avalanches of deception.

"We'll leave you alone now," Mum said. "I'm sure you've been given plenty of work to be doing over Christmas?"

"Uh-hm," I agreed.

I stay sat up in my bed until they left, closing the

door behind them, and for a few seconds afterwards. Then, I let myself sink into the sheets once more. I haven't washed them in weeks, but I've been lying in it so regularly that the smell of my own sweat barely fazes me.

Who gives a shit, anyway?

10

I know it's bad when one of the school counsellors knocks on my English classroom door and asks if it's possible to speak to Miss Lucy Brown.

The kids in the classroom stared at me as I followed sheepishly, all of them wondering what my crazy ass had done now.

Parano-

Please, shut the fuck up.

Throughout my four years at this school, I'd never actually been down to this part of it. It was a long corridor, painted happy yellows and bright blues. Feeling sad? Don't worry! Our fantastic paint-job will cheer you right up.

Along the corridor were a mismatched bundle of offices. Teachers, admin workers and, of course, the guidance counsellors. There were three of them, as our school was pretty big. One was this middle aged dude who scared me, another was an old woman with crooked glasses but a kind smile. But it looks like I'd been given the one who, in all honesty, looked a little dumpy.

Her clothes looked like they were bought entirely from the sale section at M&S. I couldn't see a wedding ring on her finger, as her hand swung to and fro, leading me to the right room. She reminded me of the kind of person who had 12 cats and named them all a variation on the word 'fluffy'.

"A-a-and this one!" she chirped, holding her arm out towards her door. "Please do come on in."

I followed her. She closed the door behind us,

shutting out the bustling noise of the school.

"Sit, sit," she beckoned. "I'm Ms. Degacey, if you didn't know. But you can just call me Clare!"

I tried to hide the grimace on my face. "Hi." I said. She was so *cheery*. She was the colour yellow personified.

We both took a seat in sofa-like chairs facing each other across a coffee table. While Clare settled into her chair, looking comfortable within seconds, I sat on the edge. I clutched my backpack close to me, huddling it to my stomach.

"So, Lucy," she started, soft. "Do you know why you're here with me today?"

My body began to churn with nerves. I didn't have a clue. Whatever it was, it wasn't going to be good. "Uh…" I stammered. "I guess I'm here because you made me be here."

"Excuse me?" she asked, taken aback a little.

"Uh, I just mean, because you got me. From my classroom. And asked me to come here." I tried to explain. It was a bad joke. It was barely even a joke. I didn't even know why I'd tried to make a joke.

"Oh," she said. She tried to crack a little smile at the realisation I'd been trying to break the tension. "Well, all jokes aside, do you know why you are *really* here, Lucy?"

I shook my head. I felt so small, and like I was getting smaller and smaller with each passing second.

"You're here because your tutor has sent you lots of emails about your university application deadline. They've yet to have a response from you," Clare explained. "Not only that, but you've also been skipping every catch-up meeting about your leavers plans."

My heart beat inside my chest, heavy and hard. Beat, beat, beat.

I hadn't even realised I'd been missing these things. I

knew I had university applications and that my personal statement wasn't done, but I'd always… I don't know. I'd forgotten, it had slipped my mind. There had been times where it would slip back in, and I'd panic, or Mum would ask me how it was all going and I'd lie. But I'd… fucking not done it. I just hadn't done it. And I didn't even know.

"Oh," is all I could manage.

"Have you changed your mind about going to university?"

"No!" I said, vehement. "No, I haven't."

I'd always wanted to go to university. It's what I'd been studying so hard for. I knew I'd never get to go a university like Brittany, all Oxbridge and fancy, Russell Group this and that. But I'd always planned, in my head, to maybe go to some university near Brighton, or by the seaside. Live somewhere new, study something cool.

Now I'd really fucked it up, by being so fucked up myself.

I felt an intense hatred. A bubbling anger. An urge to hurt myself.

I felt scared.

"Well, I'm glad to hear you feel so strongly about going, Lucy," Clare replied. "It will certainly help with the hard work you're going to have to put in to get that application submitted in time."

"What do you mean?"

"The deadline is the 15th. You've two days to get it done," Clare explained.

I felt a breath escape me after having been trapped in my lungs for too long. "So, I'm not… I've not fucked it all up?"

Well…

Not the time. Not the time at all.

"I'd appreciate you to trying not to swear, it reinforces your negative emotions," Clare said, giving me the most honey-sweet, sickly smile.

Of course it reinforces them, I thought to myself. Isn't that the point?

Besides, what's so bad about enforcing negative emotions anyway? This woman was supposed to be a counsellor. She should've been used to people using swear words as a way to express the intensity of their emotions.

"But to answer your question," she continued. "No. You haven't fudged it all up. There's still two days to pick your five universities and send off your application form."

"OK," I said. I couldn't help but let a little smile shine through. It was a flicker of optimism. There was a chance. A chance.

I could send it off, rushed but I was sure I'd get into some university if I low-balled with the entry requirements. Maybe I'd keep stuff going with Nathan until university started. Then we'd break things off, perhaps even mutually. I could start afresh. I could try to forget what happened to me and just... be me.

You could do that.

... I could?

Or you could keep yourself safe.

Or Pride could've been a one-off. I could be safe, being me.

You're just kidding yourself. You have no idea. There are some really fucking horrible people out there.

You're one of them.

I'm just trying to keep you safe.

Safe.

It sounded stupid. Was I safe? Here? Having a conversation with my own mind, ignoring the itching of the scabbing over cuts on my leg.

"You have written your personal statement, haven't

you, Lucy?" Clare asked, dragging me out of my own mind. "Lucy?"

"What? Oh. Yes. Of course." I lied, scratching my head. I'd started it. I'd typed out paragraphs, and I'd deleted paragraphs. Now, if I remembered rightly, there was only a couple sentences on it that were kind of OK.

It definitely wasn't done. I had no idea *how* to even do it. But I had two days. Two days was enough. I could do it. I could, I could, I could.

"Wonderful!" Clare said, gleeful and giddy. "Well, that's that sorted then. Do you want me to try to set up a meeting with your tutor about this? It's OK to need extra help."

She sounded like she was talking to a very fragile 5 year old. Not a 17 year old who was, hopefully, going to be going off to university soon.

"Uh, yeah," I agreed. "That would be great."

"Wonderful, wonderful, wonderful!" She swivelled around in her chair, reaching into her bag for a small diary. "Shall I tell your tutor that any sort of time good for you?

I nodded, and she started scratching away with her fountain pen. The sound of it against the paper made goose bumps trickle across my arms.

"Right. If that's all then," Clare said, as if I'd been the one to come to her for help, rather than getting dragged here. "I will go to see your tutor now to arrange a meeting on your behalf and they'll send an email over to you. You *will* check your email right?"

"Yes," I said, my teeth slightly gritted, grated.

"*Wonderful!*" she trilled. "Well then. It was lovely to meet you, Lucy. And my door is *always* open if you need to chat."

She stood up, signalling that it was OK for me to leave. "OK, thanks," I said, grabbing my backpack. I left the room, still holding it against my stomach until I was way out of Ms. Clare Degacey's eyeshot.

I started walking up the corridor towards my locker. The hallways were quiet, indicating to me that the lesson period probably hadn't finished yet. When I got the blue-green metal door, I flicked the lock with the numbers 44-24. The first was my favourite number, the second was Brittanys'.

Thinking of her made me feel like shit. Any spark of optimism I'd just had was put out by the watery remains of our friendship. No matter what happened if I went to university - if I broke up with Nathan and tried to be myself, or if I kept going along with it all - I was unsure if I'd ever get back my best friend.

The door squeaked open and I read the timetable I'd blu-tacked to the inside. I was supposed to still be in my English class and, because it was a double lesson, I would be the next period too.

I shut my locker door, hearing the lock *click!* behind it. At the same time, the bell rung, signalling the end of that period. I shrugged to myself, knowing I'd still have to go to English anyway.

As I walked back toward the English classrooms, I hoped to myself that I hadn't missed too much. We were currently looking at Charles Dickens' *Hard Times*, and I was kind of liking it, which was lovely. It had been a while since I'd taken any interest in my lessons, which sucked because I usually adored English.

All of a sudden, I bumped into someone, too busy in my own head.

"Sorry-" I started to say, before looking up to see who I'd accidentally shoved.

It was Brittany.

And, *boy*, did she look unhappy with me.

"They told me." she said. Her voice was curt and low, gruff. Her nostrils flared.

"What?" I asked with genuine confusion.

"Your parents. They told me. About Nathan."

A thousand things crossed my mind. The little voice tried to interject, telling me that my *paranoia was right after all*, but I shut it up. I couldn't listen right now.

"What do you mean?" I said, trying to stay calm.

"Oh don't play fucking dumb, Lucy," Brittany said. Oddly enough, even though she was pissed at me beyond belief, she was acting more like herself than she had in weeks. We felt more like ourselves.

"I don't know what you're on about."

Lies, lies, lies. When did I become such a liar?

"For fucks' sake," she spat, practically stomping her foot on the ground. "That you and whoever the *fuck* this Nathan person is, are boyfriend and girlfriend."

I didn't say anything. When Brittany had first said his name, it didn't even occur to me that she wouldn't know who he was. I couldn't help but wonder how much my parents had told her, and for how long.

"Is it true, then?"

"I…"

"And don't lie to me. Don't even *try* to lie to me. I have no idea what the hell has been going on since summer, but this is just…"

"Yes, it's true, OK? It's true." I admitted.

For a second, Brittany fell quiet. "Right," she said, her voice smaller, trying to take it in. "And… *how*, can I ask? Because, no offence, what your parents told me…"

"What did they tell you?"

She looked around before saying the next bit. We had a few eyes occasionally glancing over at us, enticed by the drama of our heated conversation. "That you say you're now bisexual," she whispered.

"And?"

"Well, I know that's absolute bullshit." Brittany stated.

"Oh, what, 'cause I can't work stuff out about my own sexuality?"

Brittany rolled her eyes, gritting her teeth together. "Oh, yeah, 'cause that's what I'm saying. That's *totally* what I'm fucking implying. Not that how, after you came out, we talked about it. We talked for hours that night, do you remember? You told me how you felt about everything. About girls. Boys. Being gay-"

"OK, Brittany, you can stop-"

"How you'd always known. How there was no doubt in your mind-" she continued.

"Brittany-"

"So tell me. Really and honestly truly fucking tell me," she said. Her voice got a little softer for a second, her angry facade breaking. "Are you bisexual? Do you really love this boy?"

I couldn't talk. Words twisted around my tongue, a hairball in my throat.

"Lucy?" Brittany said. "If you are… if you have realised, or if you're questioning, you know that's OK. I know you know that OK."

Whatever you say…

Shut up.

"But talk to me. Because it's about more than just questioning. You've brought someone else into this. Some innocent boy. Does he even know that you like girls?"

I shook my head. If only Brittany knew the extent of how much he didn't know.

"Jesus Christ."

"Brittany, please, you don't know *anything* about this"

"I don't need to know!" she exclaimed, suddenly angry again. "All I need to know is how much trouble you're in. Like it or not, Lucy Brown, I'm still your best friend. I don't know what pigshit you think has happened to this friendship, but I will always be here for you. Now tell me."

"Tell you what?"

"Tell me if you're just leading this poor, hopeless kid on or not!"

I hesitated. "No," I said, quiet. Lies, lies, lies.

But I wasn't a good enough liar for my best friend. She knew me too well.

"Lucy," she started. "What are you doing?"

She meant more than just here, right now, standing in the corridor. Letting the bells ring off, both of us missing our lessons. She meant with Nathan. With us. With life. What was I doing? Fucking it all up, was the answer. But I didn't know how to say that.

So instead, the bottled up emotions found their way to unleash themselves.

"What are *you* doing?" I asked, my voice getting a bit louder.

Brittany furrowed her brows. "What are you on about?"

"*You*! You! You... you come after me, start shouting at me. Talk to my parents behind my back. But you haven't talked to me. In months."

Brittany looked like her confusion was about to explode. "*Me*? It's you that didn't respond to my texts. It's you that bailed out on eating lunch with me on the first day of term. It was all you, Lucy."

"Why didn't you try harder?"

"Why didn't *you*?"

I wanted to throw something. "For fucks' sake, Brittany, I'm fucking entitled to want to spend some time away from you. I'm not the one who almost got us killed."

Everything around us is very quiet. The hallway has pretty much filtered out, kids having obeyed the bell and gone to their lesson. Anybody who was leftover was outside of their classroom doors, waiting for the teacher to start their lessons, watching the drama unfold.

"What?" Brittany said, breathless, after a moment. Her eyes were so much softer than were just moment ago, her cheeks down and mouth slightly agape.

"Y-you heard me," I said. I felt betrayed at my voice for stammering over my own self-destruction. "I never wanted to go to Pride. And you made me. You convinced me. It was *my* coming out, and you had to control it. You forced me to go and I almost died. I'm gay and I got shot at and I never even wanted to go."

Brittany stood, helpless. Her arms, usually full of heavy school books, were hanging limply by her side. Her bottom lip slightly trembled. "I don't understand."

I felt my eyes begin to sting, wetness forming around the rim. "I don't want to hang out with the girl who forced me to go to Pride."

Before Brittany could say anything, before my tears could start falling, I stormed off. I left school. And I started running.

11

I passed the red-brick houses in a flurry, the new estates going by in a slur of similarity. I would be living in one of these houses in just few weeks. Time had gone so quickly. My heart broke.

Despite the ache in my calves and the stitch in my side, I kept walking until I was out the new builds. I ignore the constant buzzing from my phone, sitting in the bottom of my backpack. Instead, I watched as shops started to cluster around me, turning regular streets into high streets. Family-owned corner shops and hairdressers turned into chain shops with glaring window displays. The amount of colours around me made me feel dizzy.

Eventually, surrounded by a small hubbub of people, I reached the train station. It wasn't the one that was closest to my house, the one I normally all my rides on. The school was closer to the centre of our small town, which meant a bigger and busier station.

"The next train to London Blackfriars is due to depart from Platform 1 at 13:05." the tannoy system informed me.

Great, I thought, tapping my card on the reader and pushing through the too-slow barriers. There were trains from Blackfriars that went to Brighton all the time. I rushed down the stairs of Platform 1, my feet barely touching the ground.

I had to see Nathan. He was the only person who made me feel safe. He was the only person who didn't question me or look at me weirdly.

And I had to prove Brittany wrong. I had to tell

myself things that weren't true. I didn't want to be the person I was becoming.

I didn't want to be leading him on. I didn't want him to be this *poor, hopeless* boy that Brittany had described him as.

I had to try. I had to stop being the liar.

I didn't know how.

*

Almost two hours later, I'm outside Nathan's school. I overestimated how close it would be to Brighton city centre itself. It made me realise, with a due amount of guilt, that I'd never actually visited Nathan here. I'd always tried to avoid it, thinking that this place would give me flashbacks, or something.

But being there then, I just felt frantic. My body and mind were electrified, buzz buzz buzzing.

I knew what school he went to, and it was easy to find once I'd asked some bus driver how I could get it. I got on a different bus and it took me to right outside the gates.

His school was big. Ornate green gates towered above me, locking me out of entering the playgrounds.

I waited outside of it, leaning on the cool metal, ignoring my phone that just kept fucking going off and off and off…

I was close to cracking and checking what it was going off for when the gates started to wrench and move. Slowly, they pulled apart. I took a step back, watching as potential was thrown wide open in front of me.

I could do this, I could do this. I could pretend. I could prove Brittany wrong. Nathan wasn't a poor, hopeless boy who I was stringing along. I could like him.

Pride

I was sure I could.

People began to file out of the gates, spilling through the open mouth. After an eternity of searching through the sea of faces, I saw him. I saw Nathan.

Yes! I could do this! Couldn't I? Couldn't I?

Yes.

I-

"Lucy!" he said, his voice loud and surprised. He pulled me in for a bear hug, his arms tight around me. This kind of tightness, something that I found so unbearable before, something that would remind me of Pride, was good. It meant he liked me. It meant I hadn't ruined it all yet. I hadn't turned him into a poor, hopeless boy yet.

"Hi," I said, breathless after our hug.

"What on Earth are you doing here?"

"I thought I'd come visit you," I smiled. "I had a short day at school and thought... fuck it. I'll go see my boyfriend."

I was lying, but it was a good lie, wasn't it?

"You're so amazing," Nathan replied. He leaned in to kiss me, but I felt a surge within that *just couldn't*. I couldn't let his lips touch mine. It was too much and I would start to panic because I didn't want him to kiss me and oh God, oh God...

I leaned in for a hug instead, swerving his mouth. If he felt disappointed, he didn't let it show.

The hug was brief, both knowing that it wasn't *actually* what the other wanted.

"Hey," Nathan remarked. "I have to introduce you to my friends. I've told them so much about you. They're dying to meet the girl that's got me head over heels."

Friends? I couldn't meet his friends. I didn't want more people involved in this than there had to be.

You can't hide from them forever.

This isn't forever...
You're trying to make it be.
I... I'm not, that's not... I'm proving Brittany wrong, I'm... trying to make him not hopeless, I'm...
You're trying to undo all the wrongs you've done, and are still doing.
I thought you wanted me to do these things!
...
Are you there?
...
Hello?
"Lucy?"
"Huh?"
"I said, do you want me to ask my friends if they want to meet up with us both?" Nathan repeated.
"Uh, no, no," I said. "Let's have it just be us. Me and you."
Nathan smiled at this, his beaming bright white teeth showing their full wattage. "That sounds good to me."
"Good."
He took my hand and squeezed it with his own, his fingers twisted around mine. "I know this place," Nathan said, as we started walking away from the school. "It's this huge park, has this great lake full of ducks. And it's surrounded by trees and stuff."
"Yeah?" I said. "Sounds nice."
"It is. In the summers, my friends and I go deep in the woods part of it and have barbecues."
I grimaced. "Isn't that a little unsafe? With all the trees and stuff?"
"Yeah, I guess," Nathan laughed. "But we've never had any problems, so, I dunno. We're barbecue pros, clearly."
I tried to laugh back. "Must be," I said. "I am sorry,

by the way, that I said not to go meet your friends and stuff."

"Oh, Lucy, I completely get it-" Nathan started.

"No, seriously, I can tell they mean a lot to you," I replied. "I... I guess I'm a bit selfish. Wanted to be with just you."

I was getting pretty good at this moseying up thing. It felt a little like I was sucking up to him, but all I could think was this was not the relationship of a poor boy. I was acting the perfect part. I could do this. I could make it so that I'd never have to hurt him by the truth. I could live by a lie.

I could.

I could.

*

During the walk to the park, I had convinced myself back and forth a thousand times. I could do this, I couldn't do this, I could do this, I couldn't do this...

And it hadn't even been a long walk.

But when we arrived at the lake, I felt my brain melt away. The place was beautiful. Despite it being January, the harshness of winter still gripping the air, everything felt so alive. The park was had evergreens upon evergreens, the smell of pine rose up in the crisp cool air. But it also had spindley, dead from the winter trees. They were dotted around, rising high above and casting spooky shadows in the short winter daylight hours.

"I love it," I said, my breath coming out in a white fog.

"It's beautiful," Nathan agreed. "Like you."

I crinkled my nose at the corny compliment. Normally, that sort of thing from him would put me in a weird mood, but I took my mind off it by staring out into the lake.

The waters were slightly muddy. Twigs and animal-made structures were made at the sides, covered by trees and mossy rocks. Families of ducks swam around, a few swans and geese slept at the sides.

"I can't believe I've never been here before." I mentioned.

"Brighton's best kept secret." Nathan said. "Wanna find somewhere to sit down?"

"Sure thing," I replied. "Shouldn't be hard considering it's the dead of winter and there's barely anyone here."

Nathan giggled and took my hand again. Taking my hand out of the warmth of my coat-pocket was horrible but I went along with it. I had to, didn't I?

Didn't I?

We walked around the lake until we found a small, secluded bench. It was on the cusp of the woods, right near a little walking path. I put my backpack down on the hardened mud by my feet. I felt a few vibrations going off, but I did my best to ignore them. I hoped Nathan couldn't hear it as loudly as I seemed to be able to.

"God, it's bloody freezing," Nathan commented as he sat next to me. He wrapped his coat around himself a little bit tighter.

"Mmm," I agreed.

"We'll have to keep close. To stay warm, of course."

I turned to him, to his mischievous grin and tried to come up with something akin to it. I was pretty sure I looked like a deranged rabbit in headlights. But it must've been convincing enough, as Nathan put one of his arms over my shoulder and pulled me in.

His lips touched my forehead, kissing it. They left a soggy wet patch behind. I felt my body cringe. He felt it, too.

"Everything OK?" he asked, his arm a little looser.

"Ugh, yeah," I said. "I keep getting shivers, though. From the cold. I'm such a summer person."

I was a summer person. Half-lies. They were only half-lies. Better than whole lies.

Right?

"Me too," Nathan said. "I have no idea why so many families go on holiday in the summer. I know British summers aren't *great*, but I'd rather go away in the winter, or the autumn, or something."

"Why?"

"'Cause then you get to be somewhere warm for longer!" Nathan said. "Think about it. Three warm British summer months-"

"If you're lucky."

He grinned. "Yes, if you're lucky," he continued. "Three warm British summer months. Then, maybe, you go in September or October to somewhere nice and warm. You'd get an extra two weeks of sun. Win-win."

"Hmm… Good point, good point…" I replied. "But a lot of people have kids and they can't take them away during school terms."

"October half-term exists for a reason!"

"Pfft, October half-term is only a week long, anyway."

"Time it wisely and you can have a week and four days." Nathan countered.

I scoffed. "A week and *two* days," I corrected. "You'd have to fly out somewhere on one of the days, rendering that holiday day useless, and ditto to come back home. Therefore, a week and two days."

Nathan started to laugh at my faux-debating confidence. I laughed along with him, our foggy breaths mixing in the air.

Things were easy when we just talked. We had stuff in common, we had stuff *not* in common. It made talking to each other... effortless. When he wasn't trying to compliment me, of course.

I didn't know. If it could be this, if it could simply be us talking and hanging out and having a laugh, I could manage it.

That's called a friendship.

I...

What you described is being friends, and friends only.

...

The voice was right. It was friendship. Nothing more.

Here I was, yo-yoing again. I wanted a friendship - I mean, obviously, I was *gay*. I didn't want a relationship with him. I didn't like boys. Touching him and being with him did fuck all for me.

But there was the other hand. The hand I'd have to play if I decided to be my gay self. Be in fear of gunmen and strangers, homophobic idiots shouting at me. People staring down the street if I held a girls hand.

I'd have to crush an innocent person. I'd have to crush someone who had become one of my best friends.

I knew I had to make a decision. Fake it or break it. I was OK with that. For a second, I truly felt OK with the fact I was going to have to make a decision, and make one soon. I felt settled and not panicky, barely thinking of the argument Brittany and I had.

It felt like the calm after a storm.

Then Nathan spoke.

"Lucy?"

"Yeah?"

"I love you."

12

I started to run.

The trees became blurs around me, green rushes of nothing. I was getting hotter and hotter beneath my layers. I kept going, in a straight line. Through bushes and thickets, nettles stinging through my trousers.

I kept on, breathless, breathless, breathless, until I tripped over a tree trunk. My palms landed flat on the hard ground, pine needles breaking the skin, causing pinpricks of blood. My wrists ached from taking the brute force of the fall, and my knees from slamming down.

I stayed that way, half-sitting, half-fallen, for a little while. Until I started to feel the cold once more. Until the pain started to dissipate.

My breath refused to come back. My lungs kept sucking in oxygen as if it was the last whiff of it they were ever going to get. I hoovered in the atmosphere, unable to take it all in. There wasn't enough air. I couldn't breathe.

The hot tears started to pool down my face, warming my frosty cheeks. I sobbed and sobbed and sobbed, unafraid of who could hear me.

I cried for Nathan. I cried for what I'd done to him, and for the feelings I'd made him think that I had.

I cried for Brittany. I cried for the friendship I'd broken, and for the lies I screamed during our fight.

I cried for my parents. I cried for the way I'd pushed them away, and for the way I'd treated when they were only trying to help.

I cried for my home. I cried for the memories, and for the fact I had to leave it.

I cried for myself. I cried for the way I'd allowed myself to think that what I was doing was OK. For the fact I'd tried to literally *straighten* myself out.

I was the least deserving of my tears. After how I'd treated everyone, I was sure of that.

I cried until I didn't think there was anything left in me, and then I cried some more.

I needed someone. I needed my best friends, my parents, I needed them both. However awful I'd been, I thought that maybe I still had a chance to make things right with them. And that maybe, they'd see how much I was hurting right now, and at least temporarily forgive me.

Turning around myself, I instinctively reaching for my backpack to grab my phone. But there was no backpack. I must've left it there, with Nathan, at the bench.

My chest lurched and panic began to try to seep its way back inside me. I stroked my thumb around the palm of my hand, an attempt to calm myself down.

All you have to do is go back and get your phone, I told myself. That's it. You can ignore Nathan for now. You don't owe him anything.

Except, the fact, you do. You owe him everything.

...

I did owe him something. But I couldn't work out what that was right now. It sure wasn't my everything, as much as the voice in my head insisted that it was. Faking my sexuality to be with him was too much of a lie for myself. I liked girls, and I couldn't keep betraying who I was by pretending I didn't. He wasn't owed that.

Even if I had convinced him that he was owed it.

Standing up, my legs shaking and my hands throbbing from the little cuts, I started to walk. It was more of a half-jog, but I couldn't get any faster than I was going. My lungs screamed, blasting fire through them. I used to love running. I could do a mile within ten minutes. I loved how it made my body feel tight and taut, the muscles underneath my skin strong.

I hadn't done anything I'd loved in months.

When I finally reached the clearing, Nathan was standing up, his back hunched over and facing away from me. My backpack was splayed open on the bench, my school books and tissue packets falling out. My purse had already on the hard-mud ground.

"Nathan?" I asked.

He turned around, but he didn't look like himself. His eyes were bleary and red, his eyebrows furrowed.

He knew.

"What is this?" he asked, sniffing his nose.

In his hands, he held my phone. It was only on the lock screen - password protected - but that hadn't stopped the mounds of texts being shown in previews on the screen.

"Brittany?" he repeated, reading from the screen. "This is the best friend you told me you had, right?"

"I…"

"I'll take that as a yes."

His voice was so angry, short and stern. I'd never seen him so… unravelled. Every word was spat, not spoken.

"Don't tell me you've gone to go see him… Can we please talk about this?...You better fucking tell that boy what you've been doing to him, Lucy, I swear to God…" Nathan read out the texts from the screen, anger, laced with confusion, filling his voice. *"You can't keep lying about your sexuality. I know it may seem easier, and I know you're struggling but…"*

"But what?" I can't help but find myself asking.

"That's where the preview cuts off, I'm afraid. I'm just as fucking curious as you, though." Nathan raged.

I didn't know what to say. He was holding my phone with an iron grip. I wanted to rip it from him, erase his eyes and his memories and have him go back. Go back to the sweet, kind Nathan I knew. Not this angry monster.

This angry monster that I'd created.

"Oh. And there's a few more, if you were wondering."

I wasn't wondering.

"These ones are from you parents. Remember them? The ones I've met? When I went round your house those couple times?" he asked, answers obvious. "Those visits where I held your hand, and kissed your cheek, and gave you jewellery? No? Don't remember?"

I remembered.

"Well. Here's some of those texts from your parents, anyway," he said. "*Where are you? Brittany said you had a fight... Why have you been skipping lessons... Please tell us where you are, we're worried...*"

Fuck, fuck, fuck. I could imagine them, pacing around the kitchen, staring at their phone screens. Irritated that I wasn't replying, taking it out on each other despite it being only my fault. Worrying, worrying, worrying.

"Do you even give a shit about any of these people? Do you give a shit about me?" he shouted.

I questioned to myself, for a moment, if he'd ever been this angry before. I wondered if I'd truly made someone feel something that they never thought they would. Betrayal and resentment. Hatred.

"Tell me what the fuck any of this means," he pleaded, but the ferocity still flamed in his voice, growling at the back of his throat. "Because I don't understand. What the *fuck* any of this means."

"I don't know… what to say…"

My words came out as pants, desperate. I was a little scared of the person before me.

"Tell me what the fuck she means when she says '*you can't keep lying about your sexuality*'," Nathan begged. "When she says '*you better fucking tell that boy what you've been doing to him*'."

"Please…"

"If you care about me, if you have *ever* fucking cared about me, tell me. Tell me what you've been doing to me."

Silence passed between us. I felt small, as if I was an injured animal on the ground. I felt like a victim of his anger.

But I wasn't the victim. He was.

I'd been hurting him for months. He'd barely scratched the surface of what I'd done and I was facing it. I was facing it all now.

"Tell me!" he shouted, fed up of waiting.

"Please just give me my phone," I gasped. "Please."

"Seriously? *Seriously?*" Nathan exasperated. "*That's* what you want right now? Your fucking PHONE?"

I nodded. Meek, cowardly. I wanted to run away. Most of all, I still wanted my parents. I still wanted my best friend.

"Here. Have you fucking phone."

He threw to the ground, next to my purse, near my feet. Watched as I had to bend down to pick it up. Pick all my stuff up.

I shoved it into my backpack before slinging over my shoulder. He stared at me the entire time. I could only look up once.

"Are you really not going to give me an answer?"

His voice was so much smaller. Tired. Vulnerable and open. It was a chance. The very last one.

But this time, I didn't take it.

13

By the time I got home, it was dark outside.

The stars seemed lonely in the night sky, fogged over with the light pollution coming from the city. I couldn't even see the moon.

The tears I'd cried the entire journey home had stuck to my cheeks like day-old glue. My phone buzzed in my hand, stuck between my sore palms. Despite the questioning onlooking commuters, I ignored the vibrations.

When I reached my front door, chipped and peeling paint, the number 72 half covered in dirt, I felt scared to open it.

I had wanted my parents so badly to come save me from the park in Brighton. I'd wanted Brittany to tell me what was the right thing to do. Most of all, I'd just wanted the people who loved me. The people who knew who I was, and still loved me anyway.

I was afraid that I'd pushed them too far, and maybe now they'd stay pushed. My old life, the one before Pride, was a comfortable pair of old, worn jeans. All I wanted to do was slip into them. All I wanted to do was be myself again.

Trouble was, I think I'd forgotten who exactly 'myself' was.

Reaching into my backpack, I pulled out the set of jangly keys. There wasn't much on there except for the front door key. And the ones to the shed, even though Dad was the only one who went in there. It was full of spiders and mould. I only had one keychain: a very scratched up picture of Brittany and I, riding a rollercoaster at Thorpe Park. I'd long since forgotten the name of what coaster it was. We'd paid such an extortionate price to get this tacky little thing.

I smiled down at the photo, remembering the upside down feeling in my stomach as we rode over the 360 loop-de-loops. Slotting the key into the lock of my door, I turned it and heard the familiar squeak of it opening.

Inside was quiet, still. The only light source was from the kitchen, glowing and faint.

"Lucy? Lucy, is that you?" My Mum's voice echoed from the kitchen, getting louder as she practically ran towards the front door.

When she saw me, standing there, stuck, she bowled towards me. She pulled me into her arms and held me, swinging me gently from side to side, tight.

"Oh, I can't believe it's you."

"Mum-" I tried to talk, to excuse myself in some way, to escalate how she was feeling, but it felt stupid to even try. I couldn't imagine how it must feel to have your kid skip school, go missing for hours, ignore all their texts and come back after dark. Lots of teenagers did it. I know Brittany sure did. But I'd never been the type before. And with everything going on, I couldn't blame her reaction.

My Dad joined her in the hallway as soon as he realised I *really* was there. He hugged me, whispering in my ear. "We were so worried."

When they both let go of me, I saw, standing behind them, was my best friend. Still in her school uniform, looking tattered and tired and sad, she stood holding her arms out.

I pushed my parents, gently, out of the way, before falling into her arms. "I'm sorry." I said to her. She hugged me tighter. When we let go, I repeated it so everyone could hear it. "I'm sorry. I'm sorry."

I started to spill 'I'm sorry's' uncontrollably. They spewed from my mouth as easily as water flows from taps, endless spouting. Brittany and my parents looked at me helplessly, out of control, as I spiralled into what felt like an endless vomit of repetition.

Somehow, they got me to walk to the dining room. They sat me down in the warmly lit room that used to be surrounded by trinkets of familiarity. The lack of it all made me want to cry. I realised, suddenly, I already was. How long had that been happening?

Brittany held my hand that so desperately wanted to scratch into my skin.

"Will you get us all some tea, or something, dear?" My Mum asked my Dad.

He looked at me, and back at my Mum, before nodding. I didn't want tea. I don't think anyone else here wanted tea, either. But there was something so inane about the act, and yet something so calming. A warm mug between your hands, steam rising and touching your face. The idea of it made me stop crying, and stop saying 'sorry'.

"Where were you, Lucy?" Mum broke, finally asking the question she had been dying to utter, in the few seconds of silence.

"I…" I stuttered, tripping over words that hadn't wanted to come out for months. How was I was supposed to say them, now? I'd trained them to keep themselves down, secrets far below the surface. Buried treasure beneath the sand.

"You can take your time." Brittany tried to comfort me.

"Yes," Mum agreed. "We can see you're upset."

"I mean, yeah," Brittany said. She nudged me a little

bit, friend slipping out of her. "Just a little bit."

Across the table from me, Mum couldn't help but smile at Brittany, too. The absurdity of bringing a little bit of sarcasm, a little bit of humour, into this felt... good. It was so stupid and preposterous to laugh, but we all started to. Once I let out a small giggle, Brittany followed on. It was the Mexican wave of laughter.

"Have I missed something?" Dad asked, coming through the archway, carrying a tray of teas.

"No, no-" I tried to gasp out, but we all started to laugh again. I fell into my best friends shoulder, let her hug me. It felt so good to laugh together again. How many nights of this had I missed? Crowded around our small dining table, my parents and my best friend. Making stupid memories that, somehow, we would never forget.

My Dads' brows furrowed, worried about the mental stability of the three women in hysterics around him.

But it was so stupid, so weird, he started to chortle too.

It took a minute for us to calm down. To let the strange wave wash over us, and for quiet to ensue.

"I have a boyfriend," I said, when everyone stopped talking.

"We know," Mum said.

"But I'm gay."

Everyone took it in. Brittany, next to me, started to laugh again.

"I'm sorry!" she exasperated. "I'm sorry! Laughter is too fucking infectious. And this is all so... I don't even know how to describe it."

"No," I said, smiling. "Don't be sorry. I don't... I don't know how to either. I don't know anything."

My throat felt dry, anxious at truthfulness. It wasn't used to being so honest nowadays. I sipped my tea, tasting the warm liquid spill over my tongue and go through my body. Despite the endless cups of teas I'd had with Nathan in cafes, it felt like I hadn't drank it for months.

"Can you tell us where you were, please, though, Lucy?" Dad interjected.

"Yeah, sorry," I said. "After... After Brittany and I... fought... I went to Brighton. That's where Nathan lives."

"How the hell did you meet this guy if he's from Brighton?" Brittany asked.

"In the hospital, a couple days after Pride. They kept in for concussion monitoring and... I was bored-"

"So you thought 'fuck it, boyfriend time'?"

"No! No," I said. I couldn't help but smile. It had been a forever since hearing Brittany talk to me like I was her friend. "I was bored so I went to the common areas a lot. And we met there. And I guess he liked me."

"And you didn't think to tell him you were gay?"

I didn't know how to, I thought to myself. I was scared.

I wanted to be safe.

I stayed quiet, letting my unspoken answers dissipate into the air. My Mum's eyes looked so sorrowful. My heart cracked.

"Can you maybe tell us why, Lucy?" Mum suggested.

I took a deep breath. It didn't help much. I hated all that slow-breathing bullshit that anxiety websites give you. It never worked for me. A knot tightened in my stomach.

"After Pride, I started to listen. I listened to the wrong people." I explained. "I heard them as they called me *wrong*. As they called me a *dyke*, and *a sinner*, and that I was *subhuman faggot trash*."

My Dad winced at the words. "No-" he started.

"I took it all in," I said, cutting him off. The words

were finally coming out of me, and I couldn't let myself be stopped. "I let myself think, for a second, that maybe they were right. And even if they weren't, I was hated enough for it be seen like they were right. Too many people hate me. Too many people hate us."

I sipped my tea, my throat drying up again.

"So I hid in plain sight. I tried to make myself safe," I kept going. "I thought that if I had a boyfriend, no one would hurt me. No one would even look twice at me."

Brittany looked over at me. "So he was your lesbian equivalent of a beard?"

"Wait, what's a beard?" My Dad asked.

"Oh God," Mum said. "How do you not know what a beard is?"

Brittany sniggered, but this time I didn't feel like I could join in. I felt heavy. "A beard," she started to explain. "is basically... Oh man, how would you even explain this out loud? It's... it's where a gay man goes on a date with a woman to appear as if he's not gay. She's his beard. He hides in her."

"So Nathan is Lucy's... leg hair?" Dad suggested.

That was it. I started to laugh again, and so did everyone else. It was so absurd.

"No. He wasn't my leg hair." I said. "He was my safety net. And it was fucked up."

"You can say that again," Brittany said, at the same time as my Mum tried to berate me for my language. I always found it funny how she did that to me, but never to Brittany, Queen of Fuck.

"What I did... What I've been doing... It's wrong." I told them all. "I feel guilty. I feel so goddamn guilty, I d-don't... I don't-t-t know w-w-what to do..."

Tears started to fall from eyes again as I remembered Nathan's face. The way he looked at me, glowing red from anger.

"Lucy, honey, we can figure it out-" Mum comforted me.

"Yeah, honestly, there's nothing so messed up it can't be fixed-" Brittany interjected.

"He'll understand if you explain-" Dad butted in.

"No." I said. "He won't. He already knows. Kind of. I accidentally left my phone with him, and it was going off and off and off-"

Everyone bowed their hands, seemingly guilty for making my phones' notifications blow up. I didn't blame them.

"-And he looked. He saw them. He saw all these texts that pretty much told him everything he needed to know," I kept on. "And now he hates me. He's so... so mad at me, and I don't know, I don't know please, I've messed up."

My tears turned into racking sobs, they took over my body and shook the Earth around me. The force of them drove my parents to stand up, ignore their slowly cooling teas, and come over to me. They held me. All three of them.

Brittany leaned over from where she was sitting. My parents hovered over me, one on each side. Everyone I loved was comforting me. Except for Nathan.

I did love him. But I didn't love him in the way he loved me. Over the last few months, he had been there for me without even realising it. I'd used him for my own selfish agenda, and as shitty as that was, he'd become my friend along the way.

But I knew, deep down, there was no way to get that back. Not now.

"You have to tell him everything, sweetheart," Mum told me. "I'm sorry, I know it's hard but you do."

"Your Mum's right," Dad agreed.

"Mums are always right," Mum joked.

Dad shot her a faux-annoyed, playful look. "He deserves to know the truth. He'll be wondering what happened for his whole life if you don't tell him."

Everyone let me take it in. My parents went back to their seats and started to drink the tea. The air felt a little lighter, with some of the weight off my chest.

They were right. I *did* have to tell him. That, I figured, really was something I owed him. I'd messed up his life and now I had to clean it up as best I could. Guilt racked me, tearing me apart on the inside.

"That isn't everything, anyway," I tried to begin. "It... it turns out that lying doesn't suit me well."

"What do you mean?" Mum asked.

"I had a bad way of coping with it."

Mum paled. I didn't want to tell any of them this part. I'd never wanted to admit it to anyone. But even now, the urge so strong to hurt myself, I knew it was for the best.

Sometimes, even if it sucks, what's best for us isn't the easiest thing to.

"I've been hurting myself a little bit," I said. My voice was small. No one was laughing this time. It felt so unimaginable. You hear about the rates of self-harm in teenagers rising, you read about it in books or see it in movies. You don't expect it to happen to you.

I don't know how it did.

Neither of my parents knew where to start, but my Mum clutched my hands across the table. Her eyes didn't break contact with mine, deep and intense. "We will get you the help you need." she said.

My Dad was looking down. I didn't realise he was crying until he looked up. It shocked me. Dad never cried. "We knew you weren't... doing so great, but I thought it was just bad nightmares and the fact you and Britt had fallen out. I didn't... I didn't know..."

He started to really cry. It set my Mum off, too. I turned to face Brittany next to me, to see she wasn't even looking at me either. Her head was in her hands, making slight sobbing noises.

I hated myself. I'd broken so many people I'd loved by being selfish and scared. I didn't know who to blame. I didn't know if there was anyone to blame.

My head felt so messed up. I couldn't make sense of any of this.

"It isn't your fault, Dad," I tried to explain. "It's no ones. None of yours."

"No, I'll tell you whose fault it is." Brittany said. "It's that fucking disgusting terrorists-"

"Britt-" I started.

"No, Lucy! It is! Don't you fucking blame this on yourself! Don't you dare! It's all those fucking pigs out there, those homophobic *pricks* who think they can say anything-"

"Enough, please, Brittany," My Mum said.

Brittany stopped, blushing. "I'm sorry. It just... it makes me so... so fucking angry sometimes."

"I understand-" I started to try to empathise, but she cut me off again.

"No, Lucy, I don't... I don't know if you do because.. God, fuck," she said. "I know this shit probably has been worse for you than me but... But it felt like you forgot I was there, too. It wasn't just me trying to help you. I wanted you to help me as well. I needed my best friend. That was the most... terrifying thing I've ever had happen to me. It probably will be the most terrifying thing for my entire life. At least, I really fucking hope it will be."

She giggled, and so did everyone else, but it was

nervous. I felt more guilt than ever. How could I have not even thought of how this might have hurt her? How this would've fucked her over, too?

Was I really that selfish? Was I really that awful?

It seemed like I had been. I'd forgotten my best friend was there, too.

And after knowing what it was like, to be there, that was *really* fucking horrible.

"I'm sorry," I tried to apologise. It seemed so limp, hanging in the air, flaccid and pale.

"I just wished you'd been able to see me," Brittany said. She was crying on and off, her dark make-up completely smudged. "And seen how much I was hurting, too. I know I never tried to tell you, because if I did, I know you'd have been there… But it felt too hard to…"

"I get that," I told her. "I really do. I kept thinking to myself, that if I told you, you'd be there. But I couldn't, and I don't know why."

Brittany nodded, her body shaking. I pushed my chair away from me and pulled her to stand up with me. Then we hugged. And I don't think we ever stopped.

14

February creeps into the air, thawing out the dried up mud-ground and unfreezing the dead trees.

"I don't know if he's gonna show," I said, my leg jiggling up and down.

"He'll show." Brittany assured me. "He wants answers."

I let out a breath. Still foggy and white in the air.

We're sitting on the top of a picnic table in the same park that Nathan found out in. The last time I saw him was here. He wouldn't agree to meet us unless it was easy for him to get to. "He's got every right to that I suppose," Brittany had said. "Even it makes him look a bit like a douchebag."

I'd shrugged to that. He had every right to be a douchebag, in my opinion. But when I told Brittany the finer details of how he'd gotten so pissed me at me, she'd been ready to kill. Behind my eyelids, closed tight shut, I can see him shouting at me again. All I could hope, right then, was that he would be a little calmer. He had every right to hate my guts, but it would make this all a hell of a lot easier if he could hold that back for a bit.

"He's running late." I said. I checked my watch. Fifteen minutes late, to be exact, I thought to myself.

"Will you chill out?" Brittany huffed. "And stop jiggling your goddamn leg. It will be fine. The kid isn't gonna turn into the Incredible Hulk while I'm around."

I sighed, making a conscious effort to not move about so much, but it was freezing. And I was so anxious

I thought the nerves in my body were going to fizzle and fry out. "He has every right to be mad at me."

Britt turned to me, sympathy painted out on her features. She was wearing what she liked to call 'war paint' today. Dark lipstick, dark eyeshadow. Lashes so long they looked like little spiders legs. Made her feel confident, she said.

"I know he does," she agreed. "But shit is complicated. It wasn't as if you thought to yourself 'oh yeah, I'm gonna fuck someone's life up. Just to be a little bitch'."

I sniggered. "I know, but-"

"No buts, dude." She interrupted. "Stuff like this is hard. You did something bad. So do other people, everywhere, every day, all the time. You're saying sorry, aren't you? Half of the assholes on this planet fuck shit up and don't even *think* about saying sorry."

"People do bad stuff, I get that," I said. "But they tell white lies. They put extra butter on their toast when they're dieting. They shout at the cat when they've had a bad day-"

"They shoot people at a Pride festival because they think the LGBT are sinners who deserve it…" Brittany chipped in.

"Oh, come on."

"No, seriously," Brittany insisted. "You're deliberately picking out random 'bad' stuff that people do that isn't even in the same league as this. And you're only doing it to make yourself feel worse."

"Well, what I've done doesn't exactly compare to someone murdering people…"

Brittany nodded. "Exactly. It doesn't. What happened to you was a *reaction* to something that most people will never experience in their lives," she explained.

"So stop acting like you've killed someone. You haven't. You made some fucked up choices after a fucked up situation. That's it."

I looked down towards the ground. The guilt still felt immeasurable, but talking about it helped. It always seemed to.

Over the last fortnight, Brittany and I had spent a lot of time together. She told me about how she'd applied to decide to apply to Cambridge after all. "I want to prove to all those competitive A* grade losers that I'm the best," she had said. I'd admitted that I'd messed up and missed the deadlines. It was looking likely that I'd have to re-do this entire school year. After all the lessons I'd missed, it looked doubtful my end of year exams would go well.

Part of me didn't mind. I was glad for the idea of a fresh start. And even I achieved a miracle within my exams, I'd have to take a gap year anyway before applying to university. It sucked, but that was the way it worked. A missed deadline was a missed deadline, whether you had PTSD symptoms or not. Whether you fucked up a boy's life or not.

"I still feel guilty, you know," I admitted to Brittany.

"About what?" she asked, eyebrows raised in confusion.

"About not asking if you were OK," I said. "After Pride."

Brittany sighed. She leaned her head on my shoulder and wrapped herself around my arm. "Yeah. That was shitty."

"Hey!" Playfully, I pushed her off me and punched her arm. She laughed and pushed me back. "I thought you were gonna say something nice."

"Serves you right."

I was pensive for a moment. "Yeah. Maybe it does."

Brittany softened. "Oh, woe betide," she said. "Look,

my darling best friend. It *was* shitty. But like I said, a shitty thing caused a shitty reaction. Fuck what happened before. What matters is, we have each other now."

"Yeah," I agreed. "We do."

"Ugh, God, stop with the gross emotional shit," Brittany joked, her smile so broad and endearing. "I'm gonna puke!"

"Don't tempt me into being more gross."

"You want me to puke all over you?"

"On second thoughts, I'm gonna respect your gross-level boundaries…"

Brittany and I started to laugh. I forgot about being cold and anxious. I forgot about Nathan.

And then he was there. Standing in front of us, watching us laugh.

"Nice to see you're happy."

His voice was dripping with undiluted sarcasm. He was still very much angry. No one could blame him, not even Brittany, who fell quiet after his quip. I felt like my voice had been taken away.

"Come on," Brittany said, after a moment of awkwardness passed between the three of us. "Let's sit down somewhere. *I* brought a nice little picnic blanket for all of us to sit on."

"Yippie." Nathan mocked.

Brittany turned to shoot him a look. She couldn't help herself. "Don't be rude to me," she said. "I'm not the one who-"

"Britt, please don't," I cut in.

She gave me her 'I'm sorry' eyes. We found a patch of grass that didn't feel too wet from winter dew. Brittany lay the tartan blanket out flat and plonked herself down. "Well come on. I'm freezing my balls off. Don't wanna be here all day."

"Nice to see you're ready to spend so much time on this," Nathan said. Sarcasm, sarcasm, sarcasm. Something we seemed to have in common, I guessed, was using sarcasm as a defence mechanism.

"O-K," Brittany sounded out. "Let's try this again."

Nathan and I sat down on the blanket with her. I was careful to be as close to Brittany as I could be, feeling safer next to her. I didn't want to even look at him.

But I knew I had to. My parents and Brittany were right. I owed him an explanation at least.

Brittany introduced herself. "I'm Brittany. Lucy's best friend. Did she... tell you about me?"

"A little," Nathan said. "But not a lot. Now I know why."

I gulped. "I'm sorry," I said. I looked up at him.

He stared right back at me, a cocktail mix of sadness and anger, confusion and hurt. He was heartbroken, I realised.

"I don't know what to say." I said, realising it was true. How could I even begin to explain any of this? Where would I start?

"Why not just... try to start at the beginning?" Brittany suggested after a moment.

The beginning. I could try that. It felt as hopeless as any other direction, so I thought that I may as well just go for it.

"Do you remember, a couple months ago, what happened at Brighton Pride?" I asked.

Nathan looked confused for a second, unsure how that could relate. "I mean, yeah. Of course I do," he said. "It was all over the news for weeks. Sometimes still is. What that's gotta do with anything, though?"

"Well, I was there."

"She was the gunman." Brittany interjected. Nathan and I grimaced at her. "Sorry! Awkward situations make me say awkward jokes! Trying to diffuse the tension!"

We ignore her, but her very unfunny joke makes me smile. It's odd, having my best friend back in my life. I love it. Even when she's being wildly inappropriate.

"I was a victim," I said.

It was the first time I'd said it aloud. *I was a victim. I was a victim of a terrorist attack. I was victim of a hate crime.*

I always will be.

"You didn't tell me." is all Nathan could figure out to say. "I... I'm sorry."

"No, please," I said. "Don't apologise. You've done nothing wrong. It's me that's... fucked up. A lot."

I scratched my head, resisting the urge to bury my head in my hands.

"I'm sorry, but I still don't understand." Nathan said. "What's the fact you were a victim of what happened at Brighton Pride have to do with me? Have to do with... us?"

"Ah, God, I'm really... not doing well at this..."

Brittany took my hand and squeezed it within her own. "You got this. Just keep trying. What happened next? Go from there."

"I was hurt, but not too badly. I had a broken arm, as you know," I resumed. "And I was being kept in the hospital to check if I had concussion symptoms. There was this stampede-like thing that happened, near the end. And I got trampled. They didn't know if I'd suffered some sort of injury, but they saw a bit of swelling so they kept me in to monitor it."

"Ri-i-i-ight..."

"And that's where I met you. As you know."

"OK..."

"And... and..." I didn't know where to go from here. That was the factual line of events. But where my feelings came in? It felt so messed. So scrambled up. My brain a bunch of fairy lights that had been left in a box for months. The thoughts had gotten all tied around each other, messed up in there, and I couldn't untangle them.

"Lucy, for Gods' sake-" Nathan started.

"Please! This is fucking hard, you know!" I spurted.

"And you don't think it's hard for me, too?"

"That's not what I said, Christ alive! I... *fuck*, I thought it would be safer for me if I was straight. OK? Is that you want to hear?" I shouted. "I thought that if I pretended to be a normal fucking girl, with a normal fucking boy, then strangers wouldn't want to shoot my brains out. Or shout slurs at me. Or just hurt me in any way for something about myself that I have *no control over*!"

Nathan was quiet. Brittany was, too. All the bravado and heat that was residing in my chest left me. Emptiness was an easily recognisable feeling nowadays. Horribly enough, so was the urge to dig my nails into myself again.

Getting out of these unhealthy habits was going to be hard.

I tried to breathe in through my nose for five seconds, and out through my mouth for five seconds. Somewhere on the internet said it helped. It kind of did, a little bit.

Sometimes, a little bit was all you needed.

"I'm sorry for bursting out like that."

Nathan looked up at me. "Why me?"

"What?"

"There were so many other boys around, I'm sure. So many at your school and stuff, or a random guy in the street... You're a pretty girl. You could have anyone," he said. "Why me?"

"I..." I stammered. "I didn't... choose you on purpose. I didn't even think to myself '*I'm going to get a boyfriend to feel safer*'. You approached me, and my brain...

worked out the rest. Filled in the blanks. It just sort of happened."

"What the hell do you mean, '*it just sort of happened*'?"

"Exactly that, I don't know!" I said, exasperated. "I... fuck, this sounds so weird... But I had this thing. In my head. Like a voice, but it was my own. Like a devil on my shoulder, whispering things to me. Telling me that I'd only be OK and safe if I... if I pretended to be in love with you."

"I don't get it. How could it make you safe?" Nathan asked. "You're still gay."

"I don't know," I said. "I really don't know. It made sense to me, my voice made it so. But the whole time it felt like I was lying to myself. To everyone around me. I *was* lying. It became unbearable."

"It wasn't fair, Lucy," he said. "To do that to me. It wasn't. I'm sorry someone tried to hurt you. No one deserves that. But it still wasn't fair."

"I know." I replied. "I'm sorry. And I know 'I'm sorry' won't do much to help. It doesn't take back what I did."

Nathan nodded.

"But you don't know what it's like to be gay, and go through that. What happened to me, to us-" I said, shooting Brittany a look. "-was horrible. What I did in reaction to that was horrible, too. I can say sorry a thousand times but it won't take away your pain. Just like the man who shot at me could say sorry, and it wouldn't take back what I did because of how he made me feel."

"You really didn't deserve to have that happen," Nathan's voice was soft.

"Like you said, no one does."

He gave a millisecond long smile. It was nothing compared to the beamers and shiners he used to pull around me. I felt as though I'd truly crushed him.

"Is there anything I can say or explain to help you understand or accept this anymore?" I offered.

Nathan looked into the distance, over the forest. He sighed, his breath foggy like mine. "I don't know," he said. "I don't think I'll ever fully be able to understand it. How can I? I can never know what it feels like to be gay and have all that shit happen to you."

"I guess."

"But, Lucy?"

"Yeah?"

"If you do one thing after all this... just please to accept who you are" he said. "Accept that you're gay. Don't fuck anyone else over because you're scared of it."

"It isn't easy. Don't you think I would've accepted myself by now if it was as easy as that? The world is so goddamn... cookie-cutter. Straight is everywhere," I protested. "When's the last time you watched a movie with a lesbian couple?"

"I don't know-"

"Or a TV show? Or a book?"

"I..."

"Unless you're seeking it out, it's not there. Not really. It's hard to find, and that's shitty. How can I accept myself when everyone around me is telling me, with these little things, that I'm not normal?"

Nathan sighed again. "I know. I'm sorry." he said. "But all of that? Still doesn't make what you did OK. It doesn't give it an excuse. It just gives it a reason."

We stay quiet for quite some time after that. It's only when Brittany breaks the silence do I even remember that she's been there this whole time. My best friend is not used to be so silent. I wondered how she managed it, with all this drama unfolding.

"So," she said. "Is that it?"

"Doesn't really feel like it," Nathan said. "But I guess so. I don't... I don't have anything else to say."

"Are you sure?" I asked.

"Yeah, I think. I came here for answers, and I got them." he replied. "I don't feel any better about getting them, but... At least I know now."

"OK," Brittany breathed. "Lucy, you wanna give it him?"

"Oh!" I said.

I'd forgotten all about it. I reached into my backpack and found the velveteen box. His Christmas present to me, the necklace engraved with an 'N'.

"Here," I offered. "I wanted to give it back to you. Maybe you can give it to someone who... feels the same way, one day."

Nathan's face crumpled, giving into his bitten down emotions.

"I-I'm sorry," I stammered, not knowing what to do, seeing him start to cry.

He tried to nod, but it was all getting a bit too much for him. "I should go," he said, falling a bit over his words.

"OK," I said.

Nathan started to get up and dust himself off. The thought of him walking out of my life forever killed me. I would never know if he was OK again. I would never get to hear his laughter, see that beaming smile, again.

"Nathan?" I called out, standing up.

"Mm?" he said, sniffing his nose.

"It's OK to say no to this. Obviously," I stuttered around, unsure of how to ask. "But I'd really like if... if we could stay friends."

"I don't know yet," he replied.

I felt a breath leave me. It wasn't a no, at least.

"I think I need some time to process all of this."

"I understand that," I said. "And I know I've said it a thousand times over, but I really am sorry for what I did to you."

"I know you are," he sighed. "See you, Lucy."

I watched as he walked away, disappearing into the February fog. I hurt, but a part of me was hopeful.

Brittany harrumphed. "He didn't even say bye to me!"

I looked over to her, raising an eyebrow sarcastically.

"OK, OK," she said. "I don't actually care about that."

I raised my eyebrow again.

"OK, so I care! It's like, dude, I'm right here!"

I gave a short laugh, not feeling wholly in the mood for it. "That was hard," I said to her.

Brittany pulled me into her, almost making me topple over. "Come 'ere," she said. "You did a hard thing. You know what you deserve?"

"Nothing, 'cause I'm a horrible person."

"Shut up. You know what you deserve?"

I groaned.

"You deserve l-o-o-o-o-ts of yummy food. I'm talking full fat Coke, one of them big-ass chocolate bars, sweet *AND* salted popcorn..."

"Oh, both sweet *and* salted? I really must be deserving." I quipped.

Brittany smirked. "You are, dear best friend. Come on. Let's get you home."

15

Every sound echoes through the empty rooms, bouncing off the bare walls. Even the vibration of my phone in my pocket.

good luck for the house move today. here if you need me. xx

...

oh, and i better get invited round for pizza the *second* you have unpacked everything. k thanks bye

I smiled. I loved my annoying best friend.

Thanks. I'm going to need all the luck I can get. Love you x

Brittany had told me off for being, in her words, "such a soppy cow" recently, but I couldn't help it. We'd wasted half a year. And she was going to get into Cambridge, and leave in the autumn. I was going to miss her more than anything. It made me feel soppy. Big deal.

And on the day of our house move, I felt even soppier than normal.

It had started to feel, after so many months of delays, that we'd never actually leave. That maybe one day, Mum would up and come into my room and announce, "That's it! House move is off! We're staying here!"

Reality, though, made that particular daydream sink.

When the issues with the buyers mortgage had finally

been sorted, the whole process became exponentially faster. We started to pack at an F1 race rate, boxes being flung into moving vans every five minutes.

I'd even gotten to see the new house. The last week in our home was also the first week we had the keys for the new house. In that week, my parents spent a lot of time over there, unpacking little bits and making it look homely.

"Don't you want to come and at least see it, Lucy?" my Mum had asked me, one even after work before she was due to go over there and tackle some boxes.

I'd shrugged. "I dunno. I don't really want to."

Mum had sat down next to me on the sofa, demanding my attention. I put a finger in my book to mark whereabouts I was. It was still difficult to concentrate, especially with my hassling Mum around me. But I was trying to read more again.

"You're going to have to see it one day," she told me. "I know you love this place. I do too. But…"

"But. There's always a but after that sentence."

"Lucy…"

"No, Mum, seriously," I had said. "Am I the only one who really loves this place? Am I the only one who's sad to leave it?"

Mum stroked my hair. "No, you're not the only one," she had answered. "How could you be? We brought you up here. You took your first steps over in *that* corner, right there."

She pointed over near the old fireplace. It hadn't burned any fires in a forever. Honestly, I couldn't even remember a time it *did* burn anything. There had been no reason for there to be a fireplace, sitting there, looking kind of ugly in the corner. But it was *our* ugly fireplace; ornate marble with family photos that lined it. Now it was empty, derelict of even the coal we put there to make it look like it was somewhat loved.

"How could your Dad and I not be sad to see it go?" Mum had asked. "Every night for a year, your Dad was in that dining room with you. Helping with the Maths homework you didn't understand. We cooked dinner, all of our dinners, in that kitchen there. Had birthday parties and Christmases and Easter Egg hunts in the garden."

Mum had pulled me in, kissed my head.

"We love this place," she'd said. "But you're going to be leaving soon. I know you're going to have do a gap year, now, but… You're still going to be leaving."

"So?"

"Well, your Dad and I wanted to make new memories. In a new place," she had explained. "We are going to miss you so much. We've pretty much been with you every single day for seventeen years. It's a new time of our lives; *all* of our lives. Let's go make new memories."

I had leaned into her a little more. I didn't really think about what it would be like for my parents, in this house, after I was gone. I'd always thought it would just be… how it always was. But in their eyes, this place was bursting to the brim with memories. They'd haunt them a little bit every day, melancholic and bittersweet. They'd wanted a new house to call home, a new place to make new memories in a different chapter our of journeys together.

"OK," I'd said.

Remembering that conversation with Mum had made saying goodbye to the house easier, and saying hello the new house a little more exciting.

One evening, I'd gone round with both my parents to help them unpack a little bit. But it was mostly to see what the new place was like.

Pride

We'd gotten in the car and driven for barely five minutes before pulling into an estate. It was a small cul-de-sac of brown-bricked houses with grey slate roofs. They all looked the same, a little bit, but every house had tried to make itself a little personality. I wondered if this was the sort of place that *neighbourly drama* was BBC breaking news to the people in it.

Oh, how my Mum would love that. I imagined her calling me, a year or two from now when I'd finally managed to make it university. She'd be moaning and whining about her gossipy neighbours, secretly loving the mystery of who was letting their cat pee on old man Jerrys' plants next door.

When I'd walked into our house, I was surprised by how clean it felt. Living in the same house for your entire life, you forget about the specks of dust and dirt. Stains that you made when you were ten and tried to fix yourself, ending up making them worse. The place was so... *airy*.

"What do you think?" Dad had asked.

"It's... clean."

Mum laughed. "Well, yeah. It's new," she'd said. "Except for these disgusting muddy shoe-prints your Dad trailed in the other day. I still want you to clean those up, you know."

Dad gave me a fake grimace and I laughed at him as he scurried into our new kitchen.

It was a lot smaller than our other one, and it worried me. I worried how my parents would perform their cooking routines together. Dancing around each other in the kitchen, the ultimate team.

"Do you like it?" Mum had asked, looking so hopeful. "We actually made them re-do this bit here. It used to be this disgusting shade of orange."

"I like it," I had told her. "The mint-green is nice.

Refreshing."

I'd looked round the rest of the house, taking in its unfamiliarity. I didn't love it. It didn't feel like home. But it did to my parents, and that's what mattered.

That's what I'd told them, too. I hadn't wanted to lie. If this whole experience had taught me anything, it's that lying wasn't for me.

I looked back down at my phone, to Brittany's text of good luck.

Today was the day I would officially have to say goodbye to this house. And as much as I understood the reason for my parents wanting to move, it was hurting.

This sucks so much. It feels like a break up.

...

Am I a loser? For wanting to cry about breaking up with a house?

...

yes babe you are

...

but that's ok. i'm a loser too. x

I shoved my phone back in my pocket. I really wanted a hug right now.

After the talk with Nathan on the park, I hadn't even tried to message him. I was surprised when Brittany revealed to me that he'd actually messaged her. He'd asked how I was. "I've no idea why," Brittany had said when she told me. "He didn't even reply after I told him how you were doing."

"What did you say?"

"Just that you were still struggling with a lot of shit. You were on a wait list for counselling and stuff. And that you were finally moving house." She'd explained.

I felt an urge, right then, to text him. To see how he

Pride

was, too.

"Lucy?" My Mum started to shouted. "Can you come help lift this box into the car for us?"

"Yeah!" I shouted back. "Just a minute!"

I take a look around my bedroom. Without my stuff everywhere, it looks so barren. So hollow. It could be any room, anywhere.

When I closed my eyes, I could still picture all my stuff. The bed facing the window, the books lining the shelves, the Everything Desk.

But when I opened them, it was still empty.

"Goodbye, room," I whispered into the walls.

I closed the door behind me, hearing the *click* of the mechanism. I used to hate that click. It always gave Brittany and I away, when we were trying to sneak downstairs for midnight snacks at a sleepover.

Now I'd do anything to keep hearing that click. Shushing it, giggling, getting told off by Mum.

"Goodbye, click."

I walked through the hallways, running my hands along the bannister.

"Goodbye, bathroom. Goodbye, stairs. Goodbye, kitchen. Goodbye, living room."

My Mum was waiting for me by the outside of the front door, a box labelled '*BOOKS*' by her feet. I knew they were all mine. I'd been last to pack all my stuff.

"Goodbye, home," I said, hand on the knob of the door, ready to shut it.

"Goodbye, home," Mum echoed.

We bent down to pick up the box together, hauling it over to the car that was already severely over-filled. I found a small space in the back, crammed between piles of stuff that couldn't fit in the boot.

Leaning my head against the window, I felt the low rumble of our car starting.

"Ready to go, everyone?" Dad asked, gripping the steering wheel. He looked into the mirror, smiling at me.

"Ready!" Mum said.

"Ready." I whispered.

Dad put the car into gear and we slowly made our way off the street I'd grown up on.

In the distance, our house became a pinprick, swallowed up by everything else.

"Goodbye."

16

August

"Do you think you deserved what happened to you?"

I stared at my therapists' face, unmoving and direct. Her name was Jaq, short for Jacqueline, and she'd always been like this. Ever since our first session a couple weeks ago. To start with, it had been unnerving as hell. Feeling her entire and focused attention on me and only me was a lot of pressure.

"I don't know." I answered her.

She looked at me, questioning. She often did this. Stay silent until I elaborated on what I meant. Weirdly, most of the time, it worked.

"Part of me believes it's his fault. The gunman's. That the people who are like me are right, that he's close-minded and a homophobe and he's what's wrong with the world," I explained. "But another part of me is worried that maybe him, and everyone like him, is right. That *I'm* what's wrong with the world."

"Where do you think that part of you comes from?"

I paused. I spent a lot of time in therapy thinking. Which was quite annoying, because I felt if I wasn't talking, I was wasting her time. We'd already gone over the fact that I'm just as deserving as help as any of her other patients, but I wasn't sure. I'd been feeling better, since the therapy and opening up to my loved ones. It was when Jaq asked questions like this that made me realise I still wasn't 100% OK yet, really.

"I don't know," I answered again. "I'm sorry, OK? I really don't know. Isn't that what you're supposed to help me figure out? Where this part comes from?"

"That's why I'm asking, Lucy," Jaq replied.

"I know, but just asking me isn't helping me to figure it out."

"What do you think would help you to figure it out, then?"

"If I knew that, wouldn't I have figured it out by now?"

Jaq stared at me. I wondered if she ever wanted to let out a big, exasperated sigh when I was being difficult. I could never be a therapist.

I twiddled with the material of my shirt. It was roasting hot in the last month of summer and everything in my life felt like it coming up to a boiling point. Brittany would be moving to her new dorms at Cambridge University in a handful of weeks. I'd be restarting a couple of my A-Level courses and applying to university.

"Lucy, can I ask you something?"

"Mhm," I murmured an assent.

"There's a part of you that thinks you're *wrong* for being gay. Is that right?" Jaq checked.

"Yeah."

"What would that part of you do if say, your best friend Brittany, was gay?"

It's like I'm in a car and I suddenly see a red light. Slamming on the brakes, propelling forward and yet, at the same time, being pulled back by the seat belt.

"I…" I started to talk, but I didn't really know what to say. "I've tried to ask myself stuff like that before. What I would do or say to someone else. Whether or not I'm actually homophobic, or if I've got some… self-hatred complex. Why I have a self-hatred complex."

"Introspecting like that can be a good thing," Jaq said, making a few notes on her little pad. "But questions like that can take a long time to figure out. Humans' brains are complex enough as it is. Throw a trauma into the mix and it's even harder."

"I know. I wish I knew the answers now," I admitted. "I mean, I know myself. I feel like I do. Mostly. I know I wouldn't hate someone for being gay. I could never. It… it feels wrong. No one can help who they love."

Jaq nodded. Therapists, I think, aren't really allowed to show their opinions on stuff like that. But I know from the smile on Jaq's face that she agrees. It makes me feel a little safer to open up with her.

"And if I know that's how I feel, then why can't I feel that way about myself?" I continued. "Why can't I not hate myself for being gay?"

"Did you hate yourself in this way before the hate crime at Pride?" Jaq asked.

I felt myself begin to breathe heavily, a sign of tears wanting to surface. "I… I think I did," I admitted.

It wasn't something I'd ever said out loud before. It wasn't even something I was fully aware of. But it was true.

"I… I've always felt, weird, with myself," I tried to say, tears making it harder to speak. Jaq gently pushed the box of tissues, always sitting on the table, toward me. "It's weird, because, I've always known I was gay. I've liked girls ever since I can remember. I wanted to kiss Anna Charles during kiss chase so bad that I actually pulled her ponytail trying to catch her."

Jaq gives me a little smile, encouragement to keep going.

"But I never wanted to tell anyone. I never wanted to come out. I just… couldn't. Not even to Brittany," I told her.

"But you did come out, didn't you?"

I nodded. "Yeah. I… I always felt like I had to, I guess. It's weird. There's this pressure around it. Once you realise, you feel like you're in one of those pressure chambers. And all the air is getting denser and denser, and you're getting more and more squished down. You can't breathe. And the only way to release the pressure is to tell someone."

"So that's what it felt like for you, then? A pressure to come out?"

"Yeah," I confirmed. "So I did. And it felt like I was right about the pressure because everyone, like, knew already. At least, that's what Brittany said. That they were all waiting for me to tell them."

Jaq did that thing again. Where she waited, causing a deliberate awkward kind of silence just so that I'd talk again. In our first couple of sessions, I tried to wait her out, see how long she'd go like that. But she always waited. Waited until I was ready.

It turned out I appreciated it. Being given the time to open up. And after a few moments, once my tears had subsided, I found myself talking again.

"I wish I knew why I've always felt unhappy that I'm gay," I told her. "I'm not homophobic. It doesn't make any sense. It makes things even more complicated."

"Even more complicated? What do you mean by that, Lucy?" Jaq asked.

"I mean, like… Being gay isn't straightforward. Excuse the bad pun," I said. "But, anyway, I just mean that it isn't easy. You grow up and everyone's talking about the *boys* they have a crush on. You get older and everyone's thinking about what *boy* is gonna ask them to prom. All the meanwhile, you're there, sitting in your bedroom watching *The Breakfast Club* and trying to figure out why Molly Ringwalds' lipstick trick is turning you on so much."

I saw as Jaq smiled again. I couldn't help but smile with her. Getting things like this off my chest made stuff lighter to carry. Talking about it, unpacking the suitcase inside my head, made it easier to see what was in it and figure it out why it was there.

"It's… it's unfair that I've had to spend so long figuring stuff out. It isn't easy for me, like it is them. And it shouldn't be that way. It just shouldn't. It *sucks* that people like me, and everyone else in the LGBT community has to spend so many unhappy years getting their shit together. While all the others just… already have it together. And can live."

I fell quiet, sinking into my armchair. Lolling my head back, I let out a long groan.

"I fucking hate it." I said.

"Do you hate *it*, or do you hate actually being gay?"

"I guess I hate it. Whatever 'it' is. The world. Society. Heteronormativity," I tried to explain. "Maybe 'it' is the reason I think I hate myself. Maybe it made *me* hate myself. I don't know. All I know… is that I'm tired of living like this. Tired of hating what I'm not, rather than loving what I am."

Jaq smiles affirmatively before giving me the five minute warning that our session was going to end soon. "Have you ever thought of trying to help?" she kept going.

"Help what?" I asked.

"Other people like yourself. Others who may be struggling with a world that tells them what to be and what to think, when they're thinking something different."

I snorted. "How would I even go about helping

other people?"

"You could find some local LGBT charities to volunteer with, maybe. Be face to face with some of the youth, help them understand themselves."

I considered this. "I dunno," I said. "I can barely understand *my*self."

"Well… have you ever thought about writing it out?" Jaq suggested.

"Writing what out?"

"What happened to you. What you did. How you overcame it."

"Haven't overcome it yet, Doc." I joked.

"Well," Jaq smiled. "Over*coming* it, then."

I tossed the idea over in my mind. Writing it out? I'd never really written. I loved books. On holidays, I'd get through pages after pages, lying in the sun. Or in the rain, if we'd gone camping that year.

But I'd never thought about writing.

"That's our session over today, Lucy," she informed me. "You've made some excellent progress today, you know? I want you to feel proud of yourself."

"Yeah, yeah."

"Honestly, Lucy, I want you to feel proud of yourself. Take that introspective lense and keep looking into yourself," Jaq instructed me. "Think of it as homework!"

"Man, here I was thinking it was the summer holidays and I didn't *have* homework," I tried to joke.

Jaq just smiled. I could never be a therapist, I thought to myself. Not enough being able to laugh.

"See you next week," Jaq said. "Same time, same place."

"Same time, same place." I confirmed.

I walked out the hospital building and back towards

the centre of town. Sometimes, Mum would drive me to my sessions. But lately I'd been trying to take the bus more, get out more. Do more. I'd lived in this same town for my entire life and I barely knew my way around. Getting outside was refreshing, and in the summer, simply beautiful. I'd found out that walking often made my head feel a little clearer. Whenever I had bad urges to hurt myself, or my voice tried to talk to me, I'd try to take a walk.

Sunshine poured on my face as I walked down the streets. I didn't even have to use Google Maps to work out my way anymore.

I reached into my pocket and turned my phone back on, wanting to text Brittany.

My therapist asked me what I thought about writing stuff down. About what happened. What do you think?

...

if you think it'll help babe then I'm on board all the way. supportive best friend train, arriving at platform Lucy

I smiled to myself. As I walked, I pulled up a couple of tabs on my phone's search engine for LGBT charities. Even if I didn't volunteer at some, maybe I could go to a couple of events if they had any on. It would be hard. More than hard. Fucking terrifying.

But maybe I could. One day, maybe I could do that.

Back in my pocket, my phone vibrated again. I thought it was going to be Brittany, double-texting me, but it wasn't.

On the screen, his name stood out like a beacon light. Nathan Huxley.

hey. just wanted to see how ur doing? hope ur well.

...

that seemed blunt, god, let me add a smiley face :) lol

I flickered.

Maybe there was a chance I could still get my friend back. Maybe he really did just need some time.

I stand against the pole of the bus stop, wanting to audible groan at the coolness the metal was giving off. It felt so nice against my sweaty skin.

Warmth washed over me as I waited. I didn't know what I would do. If I would volunteer, or become a big part of the LGBT community, or maybe I'd even write my story out.

I had no idea, but I was hopeful.

I was going to be OK.

If you have been affected by any of the issues raised within this book, or are struggling, please consider contacting any of the following organisations:

- **The Samaritans** (a confidential, 24/7 helpline to talk about anything at all): call on 116 123, visit the website samaritans.org

- **The Mix** (a helpline for under 25s): call on 0808 808 4994, visit the website themix.org.uk

- **Mind** (mental health support and helpline): call 0300 123 3393, text 86463, visit the website mind.org.uk

- **Switchboard** (an LGBT+ helpline): call 0300 330 0630, e-mail chris@switchboard.lgbt, visit the website switchboard.lgbt

ABOUT THE AUTHOR

Leona Storey (yes, that is her real name, thank you very much) has been writing stories ever since she could hold a pen. She is currently studying to get her MA in Creative Writing at the University of Manchester.

PRIDE is her debut novel.

Follow her on Twitter for updates on her future writing endeavours:
@leonareads

CPSIA information can be obtained
at www.ICGtesting.com
Printed in the USA
BVHW032009020620
580800BV00001B/8